A Dragon's Curse

THE HIDDEN REALM - BOOK TWO

USA TODAY BESTSELLING AUTHOR

HEATHER RENEE

ISBN: 979-8392311439

Line Editing and Proofing: Jamie from Holmes Edits

Cover: JoY Cover Designs

Illustrations: Art by Kalynne and Samaiya Art

Contents

DRAGO
THE DARK FOREST
CILLIAN'S HOUSE
NANNIO'S HOUSE
ROCK POINT
THE HIDDEN REALM

Chapter One

CILLIAN

My chest was burning from the inside out, crippling my body and forcing me to slam on the brakes. This was the furthest I'd been from Dawsyn since finding her, and while I'd been feeling a tug back toward her this entire time, nothing had ever come close to this sort of agony.

If I hadn't known better, I would have sworn that someone was stabbing my heart with a branding iron. Sweat pooled around my forehead and neck, and my eyes squeezed closed as I tried to breathe through whatever the fuck this was.

Without looking, I reached over to the center console and grabbed my phone from the cupholder. I had to call Dawsyn. I had to hear her voice, but even as I thought the words, my dragon's essence thrashed around inside me.

He didn't agree, and his panic was what had me turning around before, wasting time. I wouldn't do that again. Not when I was only thirty minutes from the entry point to Drago.

Forcing my eyes open again, I called Dawsyn on the number she'd called me from earlier. Each ring was like another dagger to my heart, and when her voicemail picked up, I stopped breathing entirely.

Fuck! Where was my mate?

I opened the school app, knowing some of the students listed their phone numbers in the directory. As I began scrolling for River's, the fiery pain suddenly ceased, replaced by a hollowness I didn't understand.

My fingers grasped at my chest as if I could tangibly touch what was missing. Then I realized it wasn't just the pain that had disappeared.

The connection to Dawsyn. It was gone. The tether that constantly pulled me toward my mate was no longer inside me.

Emotions burned at my eyes and throat. Something had happened to her. She wouldn't have told me all those things earlier and then found a way to break our bond. I might not have known Dawsyn well, but she wasn't *that* cruel.

I found River's number and called him next. Again, no answer. I called Dawsyn a second time. Same thing.

"What the fuck is happening?" I snarled into the empty cab of the truck.

I tried each of them once more before deciding to turn around. Every breath burned through my lungs as I prayed and hoped with everything I had in me that Dawsyn would answer the damn phone.

It was a six-hour drive at minimum back to the school, and that was if I drove much faster than I was supposed to. I couldn't not know if she was okay for that long. I couldn't wait to know why the fuck I no longer sensed the bond to her pulsing inside me.

"Cillian?" another woman answered Dawsyn's phone after I'd already been on the road for a good fifteen minutes and called at least ten times.

"Who the fuck is this?" I snarled.

"It's Justine."

"Where is Dawsyn?" I demanded, my teeth clenched and fingers wrapped tightly around the phone.

She hesitated in answering, and as I started to growl into the speaker, she finally replied, "I don't know. Her door was busted, and the window is open. There's blood on the ground, and her phone is here. I can't get a hold of her or River. I came by to check on them when River didn't show up for class."

I took one ragged breath, but that did nothing for my pissed-the-fuck-off tone. "Listen to me carefully, Justine. I need you to scent the room and tell me what you smell. What doesn't belong?"

"The blood isn't just Dawsyn's," she answered right away. "I can't tell what it's from, though. It could be an animal, maybe?"

Or it could be another fucking dragon shifter.

"What else?" I asked.

"Just hints of her, River, you, and someone else," she replied. "A powerful witch. Do you think a witch took her?"

No, but I didn't tell her that. Given what Beatrix was researching, I didn't think she'd appreciate me telling anyone that she was at the academy with us earlier that day.

"Track River," I said. "If he didn't show up for class, maybe something happened to him and Dawsyn took off after him. She never would have willingly let someone else take her."

At least I hoped to fuck not. Not after the warnings Beatrix gave us to stay in the dorm.

"Besides the tiny drops of blood and open window, there doesn't appear to have been a struggle like I'd expect if Dawsyn was taken against her will," she said. "Maybe you're right. She's probably just with River."

She better fucking be, I thought. Not because I wanted to control her, but the thought of someone else having her... I couldn't even let the thought finish without scales pushing through my skin.

"I'm not near the academy," I said. "I was supposed to be gone for a few days, but I'm going to head back now. Call me the second you find anything else and text me from your phone. If you take Dawsyn's and she returns, she won't be able to call any of us."

"Good idea," she replied. "I'll get back to you soon."

I ended the call and let out a guttural roar into the cab of the truck while squeezing the steering wheel.

"Damn it," I snarled. "If this is the universe telling me that I need to choose between Dawsyn and saving my realm, I fucking choose her. I'll choose her every damned time. Now, give her back to me!"

Several deep breaths later, I didn't feel even the slightest bit better, but that didn't mean I could sit there and stew.

I pulled the truck back onto the highway and cut across the grassy center divider to turn back around.

I'd find my mate, figure out what the fuck happened to our bond, and burn anyone to ash that was responsible.

There was no fucking doubt about that. Not anymore. Dawsyn was my life now. Everything else meant nothing to me without her.

Chapter Two

DAWSYN

I couldn't stop pawing at my chest. The emptiness there was slowly killing me, taking away all my rage and replacing it with a soul-deep sorrow. Not feeling Cillian inside me was unnatural, even if we'd only had the connection for two weeks.

He'd been mine. I never should have thought I'd be better off without him. This had to be the Moon Goddess punishing me for trying to reject the mate bond she'd gifted me with.

Your reluctance wouldn't have changed our scenario, my wolf said compassionately. *Even if you'd accepted him right away, without having completed the bond, something you shouldn't have felt rushed to do, we'd still have ended up right here.*

While I knew she was right—technically—it was hard to relieve myself of the guilt coursing through me. Though, just because I thought I deserved this sort of heart-shattering pain didn't mean I was giving up.

I still had hope that Cillian would find me in Drago.

He'd figure out I was there and wouldn't give up on getting me back. Once we were back together, I had faith that we could stop Knox from doing whatever he thought he was going to do.

Yet...Cillian didn't even know his brother existed. Though that was a problem, I had to worry about it later. Right then, I needed to focus on River. I'd traded everything for my best friend's life, and it was time to make sure Knox kept up with his end of our deal.

The sinister dragon shifter drove us to an empty house in the first town south of the academy. It was a single-story, grey, nondescript home. No flowers, no grass. Essentially, no life anywhere.

Except for inside.

I could scent River as soon as Knox pulled up in front of the house, but I had a feeling that was because my best friend had been bleeding for some time, which had my own blood boiling.

I was out of the car first and storming toward the front. Just as I lifted my foot to kick the door in, Knox clicked his tongue at me.

"I wouldn't do that if I were you," he warned.

"And why the fuck not?" I countered without turning back toward him.

"You certainly have a mouth on you."

My body shuddered just hearing the smirk in his words.

He continued, "There's a warlock inside that house, and if I don't enter first, he's going to hurt you to the point you wish you were dead. Only, you won't die. I won't let that happen. At least, not until you've served your purpose."

I clenched my hands at my sides and stepped back to wait for the psychotic dragon to go through the door first.

My desperation to get eyes on River and make sure he was going to be okay would not be the thing that got him killed. Not after all I'd sacrificed.

The mere thought of what I'd done had my heart splintering, feeling as if tiny shards were coursing through my veins, slicing me a million times over.

Cillian.

I hoped he wasn't hurting like I was and that he knew I'd had no other choice. Most importantly, I hoped he could find a way to forgive me once I got out of this mess.

Knox brushed past me, his shoulder brushing against mine and making the forced connection between us flutter. Vomit rose up my throat, and I spit it out behind me with a gag.

There were no forced feelings of want with a chosen mate. There was no greater force at play that increased my attraction to this man. No, when a bond was created instead of being fated, any feelings shared prior to the bond between the chosen mates remained. A blessing for which I was currently thankful.

If tying myself to him had changed my instant hatred for this man, I had no clue what I would have done.

Knox opened the front door slowly, blocking my view. It took everything in me not to punch his spine and barrel through, but I'd made the choice to obey this dragon shifter for River. I wouldn't fuck things up when I was so close to making sure he was okay.

What felt like several minutes later, but was probably only a handful of seconds, Knox moved out of my way. In the center of the barren living room sat an unconscious River, bound to a chair with chains that appeared to be burning his skin.

"Riv," I whispered, nearly dropping to my knees before I swirled my head around to glare at Knox. "I agreed to your asinine request. Why isn't he healed yet?"

"Because I don't trust you," he replied casually.

"Yeah? Right the fuck back at you." I sneered. "Can I touch him?"

The dragon shifter waved his hand flippantly, then said, "Remove the restraints."

I'd thought he was talking to me, but then the masked man I'd seen in the picture of River that Knox had showed me back at the dorm stepped into the room from the hallway on the left. He kept his eyes averted and had some sort of shield over himself.

Stupidly smart warlock. If I couldn't scent him with my wolf, then I couldn't track him later to rip his head off. Not that I wouldn't still try. Someone would know something, and I'd fucking find out. Nobody touched my family and got away with it.

Even if River and I weren't blood or pack family, he was just as important to me. These men were fools to believe they'd get away with this, but I'd let them think what they wanted for the time being.

Suddenly, I was able to smell something different in the room. It appeared the warlock's shield couldn't block his magic from me when he was forced to use it.

I won't forget that scent, my wolf growled with a promise I knew she'd keep.

She'd been quiet since the bond to Cillian was

shattered, but I knew she was just as furious as I was. Together, we'd find our vengeance, just as soon as we made sure everyone we loved was safe.

We need to find out what Knox has planned, my wolf added. *We're in it this far. Might as well play the game.*

She had a point. I didn't like it, but I agreed. As long as I didn't have to let Knox put his hands on me.

Fuck. What if the bond triggered a heat? Even though I hated him, I wouldn't be able to deny allowing him to ease the pain of a heat. If that happened, I had no doubt that I would wish I was dead and that Cillian would never forgive me.

Moon Goddess, please don't be that cruel, I begged.

The warlock stepped away from River, but before he could get too far, I said, "Heal him."

Knox chuckled. "You're in no place to make demands, Little Wolf."

I swirled around, and a rumble echoed from my chest and around the room. "That's where you're wrong, Knox. You might hold River's life over my head, but that can only last for so long. Either he'll be safe, or he'll be dead and you'll lose all your leverage. I've played nice, but don't fucking push me right now if you want my compliance to continue."

His eyes widened briefly, but he wiped the surprise quickly from his face. "An alpha female. I didn't expect that." His eyes cut to the warlock. "Very well. Heal the boy."

River wasn't a boy, but Knox could have the insult. All I cared about was that he knew I was right. Of course I wanted to keep River alive, but holding his life over me couldn't be Knox's endgame. It wouldn't work forever. There had to be something more. Just like my wolf had said, we needed to find out what that something was.

River groaned in the chair as the chains fell to the floor. Dried blood still covered him, and there was bruising around his face, but he was waking up. I had to find a way to ignore everything else.

"River?" I pleaded, gently touching his face and pushing my alpha energy to him. "Wake up."

A moan sounded from between his busted lips, and his eyes finally blinked open, but they weren't able to focus on me before closing again.

"I said to heal him," I demanded without tearing my gaze away from my best friend.

"He's healed enough to prove he'll live," Knox answered. "His wolf will do the rest. Now, say your goodbyes. It's time for us to go."

"Where?" I asked, still silently pleading with River to wake fully before I was forced to leave his side.

"To Drago," he replied. "There is still much to do before our big reveal. Claiming you was only a small part of the plan."

My shoulders shuddered when he mentioned claiming me. The disgust inside my heart only continued to grow with every passing second, but at least River was okay.

His heartbeat was growing stronger, which at least relieved some of my worries.

"How will I know the warlock won't kill him once we leave?" I asked, this time turning to look up and face the dragon shifter.

He stared directly into my eyes. "You're my mate now, Dawsyn. If I make you a promise, I intend to keep it."

I was tempted to vomit on his feet but refrained. If he was going to hand me an olive branch, I'd accept it. For now.

My attention went back to River. He was still unconscious, but the color in his face was getting back to normal and his breathing was even. I got up from my knees and kissed his forehead. "I love you, Riv. Please don't blame yourself, and tell...*them* I'm sorry."

Knox grabbed my wrist and jerked me against my chest. "We're done here." He snapped his fingers at the warlock. "Get us to the portal."

Cillian could be there, my wolf said. *He was close enough. The timing could be right.*

Something told me we weren't getting that lucky, but I'd stay alert regardless.

The faceless warlock used more of his magic this time, and he put his hands in front of him to open the portal. His black sleeve separated from the gloves he was wearing, revealing a star of sorts. Almost like there were several stars overlapping each other, but the points never lined up.

At least I had something else to go on when I went after him later.

The portal widened, and Knox placed his hand on my lower back, branding me with his touch. This brand wasn't filled with affection like it had been with Cillian. This was repulsive and rancid, making my stomach churn.

We stepped through the portal, and the temperatures instantly dropped. My shoulders curved in on themselves.

My spine ached from my muscles tensing. Hell, it was literally freezing out here.

It wasn't snowing, but there was fresh powder on the ground and covering the tall pines around the corner of what I assumed to be a mountain. Though, I still had no clue where we were.

The warlock stepped through the portal to stand next to Knox, and I was suddenly intrigued about him joining us. Cillian had said only those mated to a dragon or with dragon blood could enter through the portal, so who the hell was this guy?

"Go back to..." Knox trailed off, seemingly considering his words because of my presence, "—where you were waiting for me before. Don't go near the academy again unless I need you to. We don't need you getting us caught."

The warlock nodded. Instead of opening a portal this time, he disappeared into thin air, assumingly teleporting to where Knox had been talking about.

It's interesting that he never spoke, my wolf said.

Interesting indeed.

My body shivered and teeth chattered. The frigid air was making it hard for me to think or move, but I wasn't completely out of it.

Cillian wasn't here, and there were no other footprints in the snow, meaning he hadn't gotten here yet. He must have turned around when our connection was shattered. An understandable but frustrating fact.

Still, that didn't mean he wouldn't put the pieces together once River woke. I had to leave him a sign.

Before Knox could grab me again, I ripped a piece of my

red shirt and let it drop to the ground before placing my shoe over it.

Someone would find it, and they'd know where I was. Worse, they'd know I was bonded to a dragon.

Fuck. The pressure on my chest—the ache there from imagining what this was doing to Cillian—nearly suffocated me.

Knox had the portal to Drago opened and reached for me again, this time digging his fingers into my bicep. "This might hurt a little the first time."

Nothing would hurt me as badly as shattering the bond already had, but I merely nodded in understanding.

He walked us into a rock that had a slight shimmer over it in the form of an oval doorway. Barely perceptive to the normal eye, but not hard to miss if you were looking for it.

He pushed me forward, but kept a tight hold on my arm. As soon as my outreached hand touched the opening, the rest of my body was jerked forward.

My eyes were forced closed from the unexpected jolt, and it felt as if thousands of needles were being stabbed into every inch of my body.

Heat covered my skin, and I forced my eyes open again. They blinked several times until the world around me came into focus.

My heart broke again for Cillian. It was so much worse than he'd described.

There were plumes of smoke everywhere over the town that was just several miles ahead of us. The sky was dark, though it should have been the middle of the day—at least if time was similar here to back home—and the air was sweltering. It was a sharp contrast to where we'd just come from.

My skin was already sticky from the increased temperatures, and my hair plastered to my neck and back.

One of the taller buildings that appeared to be on fire began crumbling to the ground, and I briefly covered my mouth with my hand at the travesty, hoping like hell nobody had been inside it.

What was once probably an enchanting realm was dying right before my eyes, and it didn't seem as if there was a damn thing anyone could do about it.

No wonder Cillian had been so focused on finding that spell to stop this destruction. I suddenly felt the same way.

"This way," Knox grumbled, grabbing me again.

I quickened my pace, so he wouldn't feel the need to pull on me. "Where are we going?"

He didn't answer, but that wasn't going to work for me. If I was going to survive being here for any length of time without Cillian, then I needed to get something out of this whole situation.

"I've done everything you've asked with little resistance," I said. "The least you could do is answer my questions."

His responding laugh was dark yet short. "The least I could do was let your friend live."

I'd already pointed out that his leverage with that only went so far, but I also wasn't stupid enough to believe that his promise to let River live had any true weight to it. I wouldn't push the dragon shifter as much as I wanted, but that didn't mean I was giving up my quest for information.

"Fair enough," I said. "I guess you're okay with your mate despising you, then."

His lips curved into a smirk. "The line is rather blurred between love and hate. The more you hate me, the more you're bound to love me. I've waited this long to get what I want. I can wait for you."

"And what is it that you want?" I asked as we walked east, heading toward a shadowy forest.

"Wouldn't you love to know," he chided.

I shrugged. "I don't usually waste my time asking things I don't care about. I'm trying not to see you as the enemy right now. Yes, you took away something precious for me, and I fucking hate you for that, but am I stubborn enough to not see I have very few options here? I can either resist the shit sandwich you've shoved down my throat, or I can lather it in chocolate and hope it won't be as bad as it sounds."

He frowned, a deep crease forming between his brows. "You're an odd creature."

"Thank you," I replied with my own grin.

If I could confuse the hell out of him, that just might work in my favor.

"We're going to our temporary home," he finally answered. "It's located in this forest and where I've lived the past thirty-five years."

"By yourself?"

His silence was answer enough. He hadn't been alone, but who had been with him and why didn't Cillian know he had a brother?

Maybe he knew Knox existed, just not the relation. I didn't know, but I was going to figure out as much as possible. I couldn't take being around this piece of shit much longer.

We got to the tree line, and as soon as we stepped into the darkness, the previously scorching heat was cut down. Not as freezing as the mountains had been, but my skin pebbled with gooseflesh and I shook my shoulders out as my body adjusted to the changing climate.

The air was thinner here, as if we'd risen in elevation. The treetops were so thick that the further into the forest we walked, the less light there was.

The leaves were a dark blue instead of the normal green I was used to, and the branches were a dark charcoal color. I heard no animals skittering about, but there were some sort of lightning bugs that glowed inside the trees. At least, that's what I was telling myself those lights were.

"How far do we have to walk?" I asked quietly, yet my voice still felt like it carried through the dark forest... Wait, dark forest? Cillian had talked about this place, but we hadn't gotten to continue the conversation because we'd been in public. This had to be the same one he referenced.

It would have certainly been creepy enough to keep me out as a child.

"Are you scared?" he asked haughtily.

Playing the damsel could make him underestimate me, but I didn't have it in me to keep my mouth shut.

"I'm an alpha wolf," I deadpanned. "Very little scares me."

He made an odd noise, keeping his eyes directed ahead. "I'll remember that."

Chapter Three

CILLIAN

It had been over an hour since the connection I'd felt to Dawsyn had disappeared. My fingers were numb from holding the steering wheel so tightly, and my head was raging. I wasn't sure what I was going to find back at the academy, and I knew there would be little chance of forgiving myself for leaving my mate, but I had to get to her.

My phone finally rang, and I recognized Justine's number from when she'd texted earlier. "Did you find her?"

"No, but I have River," she replied. "He was beaten pretty badly and said Dawsyn was indeed taken."

The growl that echoed around the cab of the truck wasn't intentional, but also couldn't be helped. "Does he know by who or where they took her?"

"He's not really coherent yet, but he said 'someone like Cillian' and something about how only you could find her," she said. "Does he mean another hybrid took her?"

Fuck. No, he didn't, and I've just wasted hours turning around. Again.

"And you caught no scent of her anywhere?" I asked before I made a U-turn on the highway for what felt like the hundredth that day. I assumed River meant Dawsyn had been taken to Drago, but if she had been, then that meant... I couldn't even think about what that meant when combined with the fact that our bond no longer thrummed inside my chest.

"Nothing that was fresh once I left Baker House," she answered.

I was going to lose my damned mind. I didn't know who had come here or how they knew about my connection to Dawsyn, but I was going to fucking kill whoever took my mate.

It didn't matter that the tether between us had been reduced to ash. Dawsyn Chase was still mine, and I would get her back. No matter the cost.

"I'm not coming back to the academy," I said. "Have River call me when he can talk more."

I wouldn't be able to answer once I was in Drago, but hopefully he'd recover from whatever they'd done to him by the time I got to the portal.

What made me most furious was that I could have caught them. If I understood what little River had said, I could have been at the entry point at the same time if only I'd stayed on my path.

Everything inside me burned brightly with a fury unlike anything I'd ever known, but this news had also put me into an odd sense of calm. I knew I had to keep my shit together for Dawsyn. She needed me now and I would find her. The rest we could figure out later.

Whatever had happened, I at least knew her heart. She'd told me what she wanted, which was me. I believed her.

That was what I needed to focus on. That was what would help me find her again.

Too much later, I was at the entry point to Drago and the scent of Dawsyn was nearly overwhelming. She'd been here and not that long ago. She had to have been. Or I was going crazy. Honestly, that possibility might not have been too far off.

It was snowing here, but there were still faint imprints in the ground—three sets of footsteps that didn't start until further up the mountain. So far up that they would have had to teleport in to make that happen. Whoever took Dawsyn was working with a witch.

I really fucking needed River to wake up and tell me everything he knew.

A flash of red caught my eye, and I bent down to the ground, wiping the snow away. My stomach sank and scales pushed closer to the surface.

Dawsyn's shirt.

The footprints in the snow didn't look as if anyone had been fighting, which meant she'd left this for someone to find. Hopefully for me.

She was cooperating with whoever took her, but that didn't mean she'd gone with them willingly.

From everything Justine had told me, someone must have used River to get to her. He was her family. I could understand why she'd leave, but who would want to bond with her? There were very few dragon shifters in our realm that had anything nice to say about the other supernatural races.

What would they have to gain by stealing my mate?

I didn't know, but I was going to fucking find out.

I pressed my hand onto the mountain surface, and the familiar shimmer of the portal door opened. Its energy wrapped around me, testing me before welcoming me back home.

I glanced back one more time, double-checking there wasn't anything else I was missing. It wasn't until then that I realized the third set of footprints didn't come to the entry point. They'd appeared and, two steps later, disappeared.

Someone had brought them here and then left, but I couldn't scent anything other than Dawsyn, meaning the others had been cloaked.

I checked my phone again. With no news from Justine or River, I stepped into the portal.

The energy sucked me in, dousing me in darkness for the briefest of moments before depositing me just outside of the main town of Drago.

Fucking hell.

This was so much worse than Nannio had described. Wind whipped around me, sending smoke through the sky and out toward the trees and mountains. Any hope I'd had of following a scent trail from Dawsyn as soon as I arrived was dashed in that moment.

The sun was nowhere to be seen, but the heat was almost unbearable. From this far away, it seemed as if half the buildings in town were on fire. Yet, there was very little noise. It was almost as if everyone had abandoned their homes and businesses, but where had they run to? Why hadn't my grandmother or uncle responded to my many attempts at contact?

That last question really only had one sensible answer, but it wasn't one I was willing to accept just yet.

My family couldn't be dead. Things couldn't have gone to complete shit so fast that nobody would have called me home.

Deciding not to let myself wallow in what-ifs, I shifted for the first time in much too long. Instead of the steady transition I was used to, this was hard and fast and painful as fuck. Much like my day.

My skin stretched until I was certain it was going to rip into shreds just before my body elongated into its dragon form.

Earthy, golden-brown scales with splashes of blue covered my body. Claws dug into the dying ground and my wings expanded, flapping abruptly at our sides.

Better? I asked him, even though I knew I wouldn't get a response. At least, not a verbal one.

He huffed and scraped his feet into the dirt, then let out a loud rumble. Smoke puffed out of his nostrils, and rage filled our shared mind.

If you can sense her, go, I said, and he thrashed his head around, confirming what I already suspected.

We knew Dawsyn was here but had no fucking clue where to start looking.

Nannio's first, I said.

If we were going to find our mate quickly, we needed help.

My dragon didn't disagree. As he took flight, sparks of

lightning enclosed our expansive size, growing stronger as we rose further into the air.

I watched our surroundings, careful not to draw too much attention, but also looking for anyone who might still be around and could tell me what the hell had happened here.

It was one thing for there to be an attack, but for every single dragon to flee? That didn't make a bit of sense.

Within five minutes, my dragon was soaring back to the ground and toward a small cottage just outside of the main part of town. It was the place I'd grown up after losing my parents and still considered home, even if I didn't sleep there at night.

The windows were dark, and I couldn't scent any recent activity. My dragon was slightly resistant to shifting back, but it only took me pointing out that he couldn't fit through the front door for him to relent.

Changing from beast to man was still uncomfortable, mostly because my muscles hadn't had time to heal from the previous ravenous shift, but it at least went smoother.

I entered my grandmother's house cautiously, my eyes first scanning the living room where there was a fireplace full of dull ash, blankets tossed about, and books left on the coffee table. I then looked to the kitchen where a plate with food on it still sat on the table and pots and pans were left on the stove.

"Fuck." She'd never purposely leave her home in this state.

Unlocked and a mess.

I continued, stopping at my old room and peeking in.

From what I could quickly tell, everything there was in its place. Then I moved on to her room.

Drawers were left open, hangers on the ground, the bed unmade. At least it seemed as if she'd packed for wherever she'd gone and hadn't been taken. Though, she'd still clearly left in a hurry and likely a panic.

Nannio? I tried the mind link for the hundredth time.

Silence was my only response, just as it had been the last week.

I exited her house, not expecting her to have left me a note, and decided it was time to check on my uncles.

As soon as my feet touched the earth outside, I sensed my dragon pushing forward.

Easy this time, I warned, stepping further away from the house. I didn't want to be completely useless when we found Dawsyn.

This shift, while still swift, wasn't as forced, and my body didn't ache as much as before. Our wings extended once again and we were back in the air within seconds.

Uncle Jerome and his mate Fennec were my only other family. I hadn't spoken to either of them since I'd left Drago. That thought wasn't sitting well with me.

Their house was a five-minute flight from Nannio's, giving us just enough time to stretch our wings and get a better look over the town.

Fires still smoldered inside the crumbling buildings. Bodies lay in the street, some alone, some clinging to their loved ones.

My chest filled with ire, not only because of the lost lives, but because I hadn't been here to help protect them. I wasn't in charge by any means, but the people in this town... I considered them all family in some way.

Our realm wasn't huge. Our clans were close. And none of this was fucking okay.

My dragon settled down in front of my uncle's house in the city neighborhood. At first glance, nothing seemed off. The house hadn't been struck with lightning like some of the surrounding ones had, and there were no signs of a fight in the yard.

Before shifting back to my human form, my stomach began to churn with ferocity.

Everything may have looked normal, but the scent of death weighed heavily in the air.

I almost didn't ask my dragon to change back. I didn't want to see what I was already imagining, but I knew I had to. For Uncle Jerome. He was my mother's brother and deserved better than me walking away.

With tenuous steps, I approached their front door and had to hold my breath. The stench was so much worse there.

I closed my eyes briefly, grabbing on to the strength my uncles had taught me to have all these years. They were the reason I knew how to fight, why I cared so passionately for our realm. I could do this for them.

Without allowing myself to think too hard, I twisted the handle and shoved the door open. Inside was a bloodbath, and I nearly vomited on my own feet.

Scorch marks filled the white walls and marred the furniture. Blood splatter colored everywhere else, and in the middle of all the mayhem...my two uncles. They were several feet apart, both of their throats and stomachs ripped open, but their hands…

Fuck.

They were reaching for each other and were just inches apart from being able to have that final moment of peace.

"Damn you, Nannio," I hissed.

She shouldn't have insisted I didn't return when I'd wanted to come back. All of this—including Dawsyn being taken—might have been avoided if so.

Whatever was going on, she knew and she'd kept it from me. I didn't know why, but I sure as fuck was going to find out.

Right after I buried my uncles. It wouldn't be the sendoff they deserved, but I wouldn't leave them this way.

Chapter Four

DAWSYN

The trees had grown denser as we traveled further. I could only see an arm's length in front of me and the temperatures continued to drop, but not uncomfortably so. At least, not yet.

What seemed like another thirty-or-so minutes after we'd entered the forest, Knox finally slowed, then turned to face me. "I'm taking you into my home. You're not a guest here. You'll have to earn that right. Mate or not, I don't trust you."

Smart shifter.

"You won't talk to anyone, and nobody will talk to you," he continued. "If you continue to do as you're told, then maybe you'll have more privileges, but don't think that just because you've done as you've been told thus far that I'm under the guise that you're happy to be here."

I was hoping Knox would be a bit more emotional about the situation and I could trip him, but it seemed as if he'd been preparing for this moment for quite some time. Very little was going to get in his way. Yet, I couldn't help but wonder how I fit into the bigger picture, because nobody would have known about me until recently.

That question would have to wait until later.

"Okay," I replied, seeing no point in trying to sway him so soon. We both knew where we stood, and I was good with that as long as he wasn't going to try to take advantage of any normal *mate* things.

If the fucker tried to kiss me or touch me in any way that wasn't absolutely necessary, he'd be seeing a completely different side of me now that River was hopefully safe.

Knox eyed me a bit longer, seeming to not appreciate my easy compliance.

Good. There wasn't anything I *appreciated* about him either.

"This way, then," he said, turning toward a grouping of five trees.

He held his hand in front of him and used the other to slash a claw across his palm. A small puddle of blood formed in the center there, and he pressed it against the middle tree before us.

A faint glow lit up around his fingers, and then the trees started to move...

What the fuck?

Bark from the five trees merged together, creating one large trunk.

Knox stepped back, and a moss-covered door appeared where his palm had just been. "Only my blood can open this door. Nobody is coming in here to save you, so if you thought Drago would be where Cillian could find you again, you thought wrong."

I gave no reply to him. Yes, I hoped to see Cillian

here, but I wasn't counting on him to save me. That I could do myself. If Knox thought I was going to rely on anyone else to get the job done, that would be even better for me.

He pushed the tree door open and gestured for me to go ahead. "Ladies first."

Now he wanted to have manners? Like that made a damned difference.

Still, I went ahead and cringed when the stairs descended. Small, underground spaces weren't a favorite of mine, but I stiffened my shoulders and kept my eyes forward. I wouldn't show any fear while I was here.

I was an alpha wolf. I could survive whatever I was about to find in this place. Even more, I would figure out what the hell was going on.

Twenty-seven steps later, the stairs deposited us into a cavernous room with boxes stacked everywhere. The only light I'd seen since walking through the door were small bulbs that seemed to be lit with magic. There were no cords or switches that I'd spotted yet.

Though, in this room, there were probably over a hundred of the little lights, making it almost blindingly bright given how dark the forest had been.

There were five openings within the room, including the one we just entered from. The others appeared to lead toward dark hallways, and of course didn't have any signs above them to indicate what else was down here.

The walls were merely smoothed-out red dirt and cool to the touch. The floor seemed to be more of the same.

Knox brushed past me, and I flinched away from him when his heated skin touched my shoulder. He didn't miss the action, which had him smirking, but the look didn't last long.

An elderly woman entered through the third opening. She had short silver hair that ended just past her ears and piercing blue eyes that landed right on me.

"What is she doing here?" the woman spat.

Her pale skin had almost made her look frail until she spoke with such venom. She crossed her arms over a red scoop-neck shirt that stood out over her black slacks.

"She is *my* mate now," Knox answered. "She's also our prisoner until I decide otherwise. I'm taking her to section four."

There were sections? That was good to know.

"How did you..." She rolled her eyes. "Never mind. I don't want to know. You just made this situation messier than it needed to be."

Knox squared off with the crazy old lady. "No, I did what needed to be done. If he wasn't coming back on his own, we needed to draw him out. Plus, he doesn't deserve her."

I snorted. "And you do?"

Both of their eyes cut sharply to me.

So much for keeping my mouth shut.

Knox gave me a onceover that made me want to vomit. "I deserve *everything*."

Yep, he was every bit the psycho I thought he was.

I tried to see the physical similarities between him and Cillian, but there was nothing there. The hair color, eyes, facial structure... All of it was different.

I wanted to know if they were related by mother or

father. Based on the minute lines around his eyes, Knox seemed as if he was older than Cillian, but those also could have been because the fucker had a stick up his ass most days.

If his mother had another son, why wouldn't she have kept him? If Knox was Cillian's father's child, had their dad even known he existed? So many questions and too soon for answers.

"You shouldn't have done this," the woman said.

"There's plenty that shouldn't have been done leading up to now," he retorted. "I guess that trait runs in the family."

Family? Was this Nannio, the crazy grandmother Cillian had spoken of?

Fuck, I hoped not.

Though, with my luck lately, she absolutely was, and Cillian was going to come home to quite the shit sundae once he got here.

Knox reached back for me, grabbing tightly around my wrist. "It's time for you to go to your room."

At least he hadn't said *our* room. I could live with a bit of solitary time.

"What about—"

He cut the older woman off. "I've gotten us this far. Do you really think it's wise to question me now?"

There was a spark of something that reminded me of Beatrix, but it was gone before I could figure out why.

"I guess not," she replied. "I'll be waiting for you in section two. We have other things to discuss."

She turned around, the short strands of her silver hair floating over her shoulders as she went.

"Who is that woman to you?" I asked once he started pulling me down the narrow tunnel.

"Nobody."

"You called her family," I pointed out.

He glanced briefly at me, smoothing his facial features. "No, I said a certain trait runs in the family. Good try."

He was either a solid liar or I'd been overthinking the conversation.

He's a sociopath, my wolf said. *You need to be careful. I don't think getting answers is going to be as easy as we'd hoped.*

Why do you say that?

Just a feeling, she replied. *Plus, it's weird that he's not using you as a trophy to keep at his side, showing whoever he can what he's taken from his brother. It doesn't make sense. Knox hiding all this time, then keeping you hidden just the same. What's the point of it all?*

That's what we're hopefully going to find out.

Though, if my wolf was right, I wouldn't focus as much on answers as I would an escape route.

Knox had said he was the only one that could open the door from the outside. He didn't say anything about getting out.

Knowing that, I carefully continued to track our steps and turns. We were another sixty-three steps from the room we'd entered earlier before Knox turned left and the temperatures suddenly dropped significantly.

Chills raced over my skin, but I couldn't focus on getting warm for long. Short doors with small windows covered by bars began appearing every ten or so feet.

I tried to peek inside, but the rooms were quiet and dark. Nothing to be heard or seen.

He stopped at the third door on the right and opened it up. "Get in."

"No please?" I deadpanned.

Within a blink of an eye, he was in my face, his nose just an inch from mine. "I brought you here, but let's get one thing straight, Little Wolf. I don't need you. You've served your purpose. I'm only keeping you now for... Well, that's not for you to know until you need to. So, don't fucking tempt me to kill you, because it wouldn't be a hardship for me. Being my mate doesn't mean your life is safe."

He paused, seeming to wait for my response, but I wasn't an idiot. I knew to stay silent.

"Now, get in the cell and be fucking happy about it," he snarled.

Well, I could do one of those things. For now.

I stepped forward, my spine tensing from the cooler temperature. I turned to ask him if I would get dinner or anything down there, but before I could open my mouth, the door was slammed in my face and all outside sound was cut off.

The only thing I could hear was the rapid beating of my heart and the heavy breaths coursing through my chest.

I closed my eyes and called on the strength of my wolf. *Maybe we should have fought harder to get away from him while we still could.*

Our fight is far from over, she vowed. *We'll get out of here. One way or another.*

Another was what I worried about, but I did my best to

only grasp on to her confidence as I searched my way around the darkened room.

There was a mattress I felt first with my shins, a single bed held off the ground by a metal frame and no blankets. On the wall next to that was a metal bucket that was thankfully empty and beyond that...nothing.

Shift and we'll be warmer, my wolf said, and I nodded dejectedly.

This was going to be a hellish imprisonment, but I wasn't giving up yet. It was only day one, and even if hope could be a fickle bitch, I was still going to hold out that things would begin looking up.

They had to, because dying in this dungeon wasn't an option.

Chapter Five

CILLIAN

It had taken me two hours to bury my uncles. Two hours of moving from their house to the burial grounds of my clan twice. In all that time, I didn't see one person. Not in town or near the trees.

Being alone and having more time to think while I'd dug their graves had made me wonder about several things I hadn't allowed myself to dwell on before. How had Dawsyn gotten here?

I wanted to believe that one of the elders lifted the restriction for other supernaturals to come into our realm, but deep in my heart, where our bond no longer beat inside me, I knew differently.

Dawsyn was mated to another dragon shifter.

As I began to put the pieces together in my mind, I didn't need River to call me with more information. I knew what had happened.

Someone threatened River. Nearly beat him to death. The only way he would survive was for Dawsyn to willingly go with whoever stole her from me.

The only thing I didn't know was who. There wasn't a single person I could think of who would go to those lengths or have the resources to know what Dawsyn was to me.

Though, that didn't mean such a person didn't exist. Whoever they were, they were powerful, but I wasn't afraid. I wouldn't stop until I found my mate and took her back. I wouldn't bow down to whoever had made our people scatter into the darkness.

I wouldn't let my realm die and my mate with it.

My fingers dug into the upturned dirt one last time, and I closed my eyes, giving my final farewell to my uncles. This wasn't the formal burial they should have had, but it was the best I could offer at the moment and better than letting them rot inside their home.

As I stood back up, my shoulders tensed. I took a deep inhale, staying as still as possible. Nothing was out of the ordinary, but I knew without a doubt I was no longer alone.

My fingers extended into claws, and I was two seconds from shifting when a force leapt for me. I swiped my right arm out and sank my sharp claws into metal.

The responding laugh was the last thing I expected, but it was also a welcome sound.

"Good to see Earth didn't weaken your senses, old friend," a familiar voice said as I pulled my arm back.

My eyes took in my oldest friend Lykem. His short strawberry-blond hair was matted and dirty as if he'd been living outside for days, possibly even weeks. Yet, his blue eyes were bright with mischief as if he'd been having the time of his life.

Fresh scars littered his arms, and his chest was covered with chainmail while his arms held the metal shield I'd just punctured.

"What the hell has been happening here?" I asked, glancing back at the ground where I'd just laid my uncles to rest. "And why were they left behind?"

Fury coated my words. I didn't blame Lykem—at least not yet—but there was no containing the rageful grief currently moving through me. A burning so severe inside my chest that I wasn't sure if I'd ever be whole again. Not without Dawsyn. Not without my family that I'd been trying so hard to save but had left me in the dark.

It was difficult not to be resentful toward them for sending me away and not telling me how bad things were when I'd never have met Dawsyn if I hadn't gone to Mystics Academy. But still, the thoughts were there.

"It was two days after you left," Lykem answered. "Hellfire came down from the sky. We suspected from the dark forest, but every raid we've done there has resulted in no signs as to who or what is attacking us. The lightning has also worsened, but everything has been calmer the last few days."

I suspected that was because whoever was doing this had left to steal my mate.

The snarl that ripped from my chest at the mere thought had Lykem backing up two steps. "What's going on? What do you know?"

My darkening eyes leveled on him. "What I know is that my family hid all of this from me. That my uncles are dead, my grandmother is missing, and someone has taken my mate."

I was drowning in ire. I'd been containing it to stay focused on finding Dawsyn and my family, but the more time that passed without them, the less I could tamp down the frenzy of wrath within me.

Energy sizzled along my skin, scales poked through, and the incoming shift was nothing that I could stop.

Lykem moved out of the way just in time to avoid being stomped on by my dragon. My roar was filled with the sorrow I'd been trying to ignore and the fury I no longer wanted to hide.

Sparks of white energy sizzled along our scales and grew in power as we breathed harder. My mind was fully melded with my dragon's, something we hadn't been able to do since leaving Drago all those weeks ago. We were one, and not having to worry about expelling too much power was a small relief I hadn't expected. Even upon arriving earlier, I'd been holding back to maintain some semblance of control, but not any longer.

Our wings flapped hard, and we pushed into the sky. Lightning ricocheted around us, the charge coming from deep within my dragon's form. Releasing the bolts of energy recharged my soul. Reminded me who I was, what I was capable of, and why I'd been chosen to go to Earth to find the solution to our realm's problem.

I was Cillian of the Silver clan. This was my home, and nobody was going to take it from me. Not only that, but I was going to find Dawsyn and rip the throat out of the bastard who thought to touch her when she was already mine.

My mate. My wolf. All fucking *mine*.

This wrath had been so tightly wound inside me that

once I'd unleashed the depths of its power, there was no containing it.

Lykem's red dragon followed behind me at a safe distance, but while I appreciated that he'd been the only one to come out of hiding for me, I didn't need him at the moment. I needed Dawsyn. I needed to know that my Nannio wasn't dead like my uncles.

I needed whatever the fuck was happening here to end.

We soared through the sky, power rolling off our scales and into the sky in visible waves. Everything we'd been forced to keep pent up for those weeks on Earth was finally set free. I'd expected to feel better once this happened, but the longer we were in the sky, the more I saw.

Buildings everywhere had been abandoned, half scorched. Houses were quiet, families on the run, and our resources destroyed.

The rivers ran black in color and the farms were filled with dead crops. The dark forest and the mountains that remained too cold for anybody to live there seemed to be the only things within sight that remained unharmed.

We finally headed back to the ground, and the shift from beast to man was back to feeling empowering instead of agonizing.

Lykem shifted back as well, staring at me with his signature smirk. The dragon was one of the fiercest warriors I knew, but he often annoyed the shit out of me with that grin.

There was little that could shake my friend. As irritated as I wanted to be with his overly happy demeanor, I was sometimes jealous of his ability to put walls up and keep out all the dark shit I often held on to.

"Feel better now?" he asked, stepping closer to me.

"No," I grumbled.

His responding chuckle didn't help my sour mood. "Great. So, do you want to tell me more about this mate you mentioned before losing your shit?"

I didn't want to talk about Dawsyn. Not yet. Not until I understood what the hell had been happening here and how that information might help me find her.

"You first," I said. "Where is everyone?"

They couldn't all be dead or missing.

"There are about a hundred of us in the caves beneath Rock Point," he answered, and I promptly cut him off.

"Where are the others?" Our realm should have had thousands of people right here in the main town with another thousand living remotely.

The grimace on his normally jovial face didn't ease the rage inside. "They're either dead or trying to survive on their own in the mountains and will be dead soon. We gathered as many as we could, but there wasn't much warning before the worst of the attacks began. Your uncles were among the first to die."

The ache in my chest intensified. "And my grandmother?"

"None of us have seen her," Lykem answered. "I went to her house myself, but she was already gone. I would have sent for you, but our numbers were already so few, I couldn't risk losing anyone else."

"How are you surviving in the caves?" I asked. "Isn't it freezing there right now?"

He shrugged and smiled again. "With enough dragon fire, anything can be warm enough. Plus, the snow melt from the extra heat is giving us clean water, which is something we didn't have here in town any longer. A group goes out every other day to hunt for meat."

Looking at him closer, I could see not everyone was eating as they needed to be, including my friend.

"So, that's what happened, but what are you doing about it?" I asked, glancing around at the dying farm we'd landed by.

This time his laugh was dark and defensive. "We're surviving, Cillian. You might have buried your uncles, but I've dug more holes than one should in an entire lifetime. For the old and young and all those in between."

My hand clasped his shoulder. "I'm sorry. If I'd known..."

"We know you would have been here," he said, then smiled again. "So, about that mate?"

Of course, he wasn't going to let that go. Though, this time I was okay with talking about her, because nothing he'd said had given me any ideas as to where I needed to start looking for Dawsyn.

"She's a wolf shifter I met at the academy where I was searching for information."

He gaped at me. "But if she's not a dragon shifter..."

I knew what he was already thinking, and I wasn't ready to rehash that rage.

"Someone took her and our bond broke, but in the process, they left someone else alive," I said. "My mate's best friend. He said something that made me feel confident that she was brought here."

"She's not with us," Lykem replied, "but she might be in the dark forest."

I tilted my head. "I thought you said you'd searched that area and found nothing."

"But that doesn't mean there's nothing to find." He glanced behind us in the direction of said forest. "We've all heard the stories about the dark magic in those trees. As we grew older, we'd assumed the tales to be lies, but what if they weren't?"

"What are you saying, Lykem?" I'd thought the dark forest was something more as well, but filled with magic? How could nobody have done anything about that all these years?

"When I've been in there, I get this sense we're missing something right in front of our faces," he answered. "Like there's a realm within our realm that we can't see, but if you're really looking, there are low vibrations that prove something or somewhere is out there."

If Dawsyn was hidden within another realm, I wasn't sure how I would ever find her, but that didn't mean I was going to give up.

"I'm going to head there," I said, turning away from my friend. "You don't have to come with me. I know you have people to protect, but I can't give up on my mate."

He stepped to my side. "You're my oldest friend and the only person I can consider family any longer. I'm not letting you do this on your own."

My chest ripped further open at his words. I wasn't sure how he wasn't losing his shit, but I'd take his steadfast support.

Anything to get me back to Dawsyn.

"Let's go then."

Chapter Six

DAWSYN

Two days had passed since I'd been brought into the dungeon of the underground bunker. Silence had been my only companion. Well, that and darkness.

Am I not company enough? my wolf retorted.

You know what I meant.

Yes, I'd had my wolf and my wolf had me, but given I mostly considered us one in the same, we were truly alone here.

I was trying to be grateful that Knox wasn't trying to get me to be his mate in the many other ways I'd envisioned, but it was hard not to be frustrated.

He'd seemed so hell bent on taking me, yet wanted nothing to do with me. None of it made sense.

He's trying to break you, my wolf said. *He'll come for you when you're at your weakest and can't tell him no.*

Like hell was I going to let him get his way. I had come here on my own—sort of—and I was going to leave on my own.

The only positive was that the cell I was being kept in

had warmed several degrees since our arrival, so I didn't have to remain in wolf form the whole time.

I laid on the mattress, staring into the nothingness around me, wishing I could hear even the drip-drop of a leaky faucet at this point.

My hands folded over my stomach, ignoring the grumbles of hunger beneath them, and I closed my eyes, wishing for sleep to pass the time by.

It wasn't long after that when my eyes popped open, as if a bubble around me had burst.

I was out of the bed and on my feet with my hands out in the blink of an eye.

A woman's laugh echoed in the darkness. "Brave girl. You're ready to fight what you do not know."

"Traitorous grandmother," I quipped in return. "You chose the wrong grandson."

I could hear her snarl, but still couldn't see her. "You know nothing about what I've chosen."

At least I had my confirmation that she was the Nannio Cillian had spoken about before, even if Knox had tried to deny it previously.

"That might be true, but I've come to know Cillian and he never would have done this to his family."

"We'll see about that," she muttered. "Take this."

Something slid across the floor, bouncing against my shoes. I didn't dare bend down to pick it up. She could use the distraction to attack me, and I wasn't going to make any stupid moves while I was in here.

"It's not poisoned," she added. "We want you alive. For now."

Oh, how I wished I could see this woman.

"Why should I believe you?" I asked.

She scoffed. "You shouldn't."

I heard a door shut and waited for the silence to return, but instead, I could hear her retreating footsteps. Then another door slammed closed, followed by several locks being engaged.

I waited, standing there frozen in place, and the only other thing I could hear was the wind blowing in from somewhere. Hopefully somewhere I could escape out of.

My shoe nudged the tray at my feet, and I bent down, feeling around blindly. There were two rolls, some sort of red meat based on the smell, and a bottle of water.

I shoved a mouthful of bread between my teeth as I opened the water, listening for the safety seal to break. Not that it would assure me I wasn't going to die from eating or drinking any of this, but it was a small reassurance, nonetheless.

What do we think of the grandmother? I asked my wolf.

That she needs to die, she replied. *She smells like death.*

I'd missed that, but I wasn't surprised. If she'd chosen Knox over Cillian, then I assumed her hands were covered in blood.

She at least wasn't lying about the food, my wolf added. *Nothing tastes or smells off, but she either didn't know there was a shield over the room or forgot to put it up. I'm not sure which is worse.*

Why can't either be good? I asked. *At least we can hear something other than silence and each other.*

There's more wrong with this place than just being a prisoner here, she replied. *We can't trust anyone.*

That I could agree with, but we were going to have to

get people to trust *us* if we were going to find a way out of here.

ANOTHER DAY LATER—ACCORDING TO MY WOLF who could apparently tell the time without needing a clock or the sun—it didn't matter that the little bubble around our cell had been burst. There were still no other fucking sounds.

I was hours from going insane when Nannio, also now known as Psycho Granny, returned. Though, it annoyed me to think of her as a grandmother. Someone who could trick their grandson into abandoning their home just so she could further sabotage things didn't deserve such a title, which was how I ended up thinking of her as The Psycho.

She entered my cell for the second time, still invisible in the darkness, and slid another tray over to me. I'd kept the first one, tempted to beat her to death with it, but decided it was time to see just how cocky she felt.

If these people truly thought they had me right where they wanted, they'd have no problem telling me things they didn't want others to know.

"Why did you turn on Cillian?" I asked, picking up the tray and biting into the roll.

She didn't answer at first. I heard the hinges on the door creak, thinking she was going to leave, but then she paused. "I didn't turn on him."

I snorted and nearly choked on the bread. "Right. Because when you sent him to another world, stopped talking to him, and then stole his mate, that was you being on his side."

"I didn't steal you."

"Yet, you also haven't let me out. Guilty by association." At least, that was what I was convinced of.

She didn't respond, so I asked another question. "Why doesn't Cillian know about Knox?"

"Because he doesn't need to," she answered.

"But he's going to," I said confidently. "Cillian will come for me."

"He won't find you, even if he knows you're here," she replied, not sounding as sure about her words as I suspected.

"Why is that?"

"Because Knox made sure of that a long time ago."

Before I could ask another question, the door slammed shut and her retreating footsteps sounded. I didn't bother to yell at her. I merely enjoyed another meal in the dark. What was the point of being pissed-the-fuck-off right now? Being angry wasn't going to improve my situation. In fact, it was likely to make it worse.

***

AFTER ANOTHER THREE DAYS, MY SKIN WAS getting itchy from not being able to run with my wolf. In total, six days had passed since I'd last seen Cillian. Since Beatrix had started her research and promised not to tell my parents about what I'd told her unless things got worse.

I'd spent a lot of time thinking about my family when I

wasn't thinking about Cillian or how to escape this hellhole.

My parents were never going to let me leave the pack again. Of that I was certain, but I was also certain that between my family—including those not blood-related—and my mate, I wasn't going to die here.

And because of us, my wolf added.

Obviously, we'll be the true heroes. I laughed. *But our family won't give up on us, and knowing that makes me not give up.*

The Psycho had returned every day, once a day, with the same meal of steak and rolls and a water. My energy was returning, and I was slowly learning more about this place with each question that I asked.

From what I could gather, Knox had created this place years ago. He was older than Cillian and very fucking vengeful. Little did big brother know, he'd just given his little brother the same vengeance.

My heart ached from missing my mate, and not the one I'd been forced to choose. Funnily enough, there wasn't a single part of me that ached to be near Knox.

I thought even with chosen mates that there'd be some sort of draw toward each other, regardless of how much I despised him, but the fact that he'd stayed away since bringing me down here proved that neither of us wanted the other.

Lucky fucking me.

It was near what I'd become accustomed to as bedtime when a bright light shined into the hallway and I heard Knox's voice.

"Then, we'll drain his blood," he growled. "Either way, I want his magic and if he won't give it, then I'll take it."

Another door opened, and I stayed frozen in place, afraid to make a noise and miss whatever was happening in a cell near mine.

"Good evening, Darius," Knox cooed. "I've come to collect your monthly payment."

"I'm done helping you," another man responded. "You'll have to kill me."

Knox clicked his tongue. "Oh, old man. Don't tempt me with a good time." The sound of a fist hitting flesh echoed through the dank area. "Give me what I asked for."

Knox's voice was no longer cordial, and my skin crawled just knowing how close he was.

"No," the man responded.

Three more punches and the sound of breaking bones filled my ears.

"That's enough or he really will be dead," The Psycho said.

Huh. I didn't realize she was there as well.

"Make him cooperate, Estelle," Knox spat, then added, "or it will be your blood I come for next."

I heard the slamming of another door, but then a wrestling sound.

"Don't fucking threaten me, boy," The Psycho a.k.a. Estelle hissed. "I'm the only reason you've gotten this far. You need me."

He laughed darkly. "I don't *need* anyone." Footsteps sounded closer. "Speaking of need..."

Mother shittery shit.

I laid my head down on the bed, evened my breathing, and turned my back to the door. I couldn't see much in this kind of darkness without ambient light, but that didn't mean the dragon couldn't. Cillian and I had never really discussed what he could and couldn't do or how similar we might be.

My door opened, and there was a beat of silence before Knox whispered, "Sleep well, Little Wolf. It's almost time for you to come out and play."

I stayed perfectly still, refusing to allow my body to react in any way, and it paid off.

The door closed once more, and then the bubble was back.

I no longer heard the sound of retreating footsteps or voices.

We were back to the dark silence, but my motivation to get the fuck out of that cell had just gone up.

All I needed now was for The Psycho to return, and I was finally going to act.

Chapter Seven

CILLIAN

I'd searched that fucking forest day and night, barely stopping to sleep. The entire area was doused in magic, making it so that nothing stood out, which meant everything had to be checked.

My dragon had flown over the area for hours, and I'd spent even longer walking through the dense trees. There'd been moments where I'd sworn that I could sense something deeper, but everywhere I looked, there were only trees. Nothing to tell where they were hiding or how I could get inside.

It was the morning of the fifth day since Dawsyn had been taken, and I was being forced to eat food I didn't want before I made up my mind on what I was going to do.

My short time with Dawsyn at Mystics Academy had shown me that my mate had plenty of people who loved her and cared about her wellbeing.

River had to be awake, and Beatrix would likely have tried to reach out, which meant her parents probably also knew she was missing. If I didn't want them to hate me more than I already suspected they would for putting Dawsyn in this situation, then I needed to let them know what was happening.

Only, I'd been putting it off because there was nothing to fucking tell them.

My mate was gone. I had no idea who had her or how I was going to find her. That wasn't something I wanted to admit. Even if our bond was currently severed, she was still mine to protect, and I'd failed.

"Easy, bro," Lykem said from across the counter. "You don't want Greta to see you bending forks. She's already pissed she had to take on feeding everyone."

Greta was from the Crimson clan. Their line of dragons were known for their tempers, but also thrived on taking control. I wasn't surprised that she'd been in charge of food dispersals when I arrived at the caves.

The plate in front of me was carved from the trees and polished by hand. The silverware was forged by members of the Emerald clan—dragons who excelled in creation and the reason we'd survived so long in Drago on our own.

The eggs and bland bread weren't appealing, but I knew I had to keep fed if I wanted to be at my best, so I shoved the remaining bits of food into my mouth and headed to the tubs against one of the cave walls.

I rinsed the food off in the tub of dirty water, then deposited the dishes into the soapy, cleaner one next to it.

Turning back to Lykem, I knew what I needed to do next. "I'm going back to Earth. I need to let Dawsyn's family know that I'm looking for her and will update them as soon as I can."

He grinned, but I shook my head before he could reply. "You're staying here."

"Not a chance in hell," he said. "You're not the only one who gets to have all the fun."

I wouldn't call telling my mate's family that I couldn't find her fun, but whatever he wanted to think.

"No." I headed toward the cave exit, ignoring the shifters sleeping on tattered blankets draped over the dirt floor. If I thought too much about the living conditions here, I was going to lose my damn mind.

I had to find Dawsyn first.

By the time I reached the opening, Lykem was keeping stride with me and staying silent.

"You're not going," I said.

Still, he said nothing.

"They need you here," I added.

We got outside, and it was time for me to shift so that I could get to the portal quicker, but Lykem skipped ahead and beat me to it.

The stubborn fucker wasn't going to take no for an answer.

At least I still had my phone. I didn't need to drive back to the academy. I could call River, give the update, and we could come back. We'd be gone for five or ten minutes.

I called the shift forward, reveling in the charged energy of my dragon as his body formed. He was in the sky just a few seconds behind Lykem, and we followed his red dragon toward the portal opening.

My eyes still scanned the area below, but there was nothing new to see. Not even new destruction. Since coming back, things had been exceedingly quiet, which bothered me and several others. If whoever had been attacking had stopped, what were they planning next? That was an answer we likely wouldn't get until it was too late.

We arrived at the portal and shifted back to our human forms, and I placed my hand on Lykem's chest. "You need to conceal your energy before we walk through this portal."

He gave me one of his signature smirks. "I prepared for this moment the day you came back." Then, he closed his eyes and a shimmer of opaque energy covered his body for a few seconds.

When he looked my way again, the cockiness of his grin wasn't something I had any intention of responding to. Instead, I concealed my own energy, noticing that the magic was harder to pull from, which meant I would need to use another scale soon to re-up the cloaking spell.

The portal before us was an invisible forcefield between two trees, one that could be sensed, but never seen. The energy made my skin itch, but I didn't hesitate walking through the doorway.

Three steps forward and I was standing at the base of a snow-covered mountain. Another second later, my phone began vibrating like crazy in my pocket.

I moved out of the way to check the messages as Lykem stepped through.

"What the fuck is this shit?" He shuddered. "You didn't tell me my balls might freeze off."

I ignored his complaints as I stared at the screen on my phone.

River: Why haven't you called me back? Where the fuck is Dawsyn?

River: Beatrix called. Roman and Cait have called. You need to answer the damn phone.

River: You're so fucked if you don't bring her back.

Unknown: I have your scales and blood, boy. I will find you and you will give me my granddaughter.

Unknown: You have twelve hours before the hunt begins.

There were others, but I stopped reading as soon as Lykem punched me in the shoulder. "Look up."

I slid my phone back into my pocket as I sensed Dawsyn's GiGi and two wolf shifters in front of us.

I should have expected this. I'd known they'd be furious, but had hoped that River would have made them understand that I wasn't the one who took her.

"Cillian," Beatrix said with a snarl. "Where is Dawsyn?"

The man beside her stormed forward, vengeance in his raging blue eyes and dripping with alpha power. The woman behind him looked just like my mate with her brunette hair and sharp facial features.

Feeling rather confident these were Dawsyn's parents, I didn't try to stop the alpha wolf as he pinned me against the rocks. "I don't care who you are. If you don't bring back my daughter, I will rip every fucking scale from your body."

His forearm pressed into my throat, and I saw Lykem stepping closer, but I shook my head, trying to tell him to stay back. Unfortunately, Dawsyn's dad thought I was telling him no.

He smashed his forehead into my face, likely breaking my nose based on the sharp pains radiating from there.

"Don't fucking tell me no," he hissed. "Or it will be the last thing you do."

The woman approached. "Roman, he can't talk if you're choking him, and he's Dawsyn's mate. He doesn't smell like her, which means he hasn't been with her. Let him explain."

"As much as I love a good torture session," Beatrix said, "Cait's right. I saw them together. His intentions were good. At least then."

Roman shoved me harder into the jagged rocks of the mountain. "Speak. Quickly." Then, he turned to the old witch. "We're still going to discuss you knowing about all this days ago."

She didn't seem at all afraid of the wolf shifter. Instead, she gave her attention back to me. "You gave me your scales and blood. I can track you anywhere on Earth, and you don't have what you need to save your realm, because it belongs to me. Tell us what happened to Dawsyn."

"You got the short end of the stick with in-laws," Lykem whispered, garnering a snarl from Roman, but a grin from Beatrix.

I ignored them and started relaying everything I knew. "River was taken and I'm assuming used as bait to get Dawsyn to cooperate with whoever has her."

"You don't know who took my daughter?" This time it was Cait who snarled.

"Not yet, but it's not for lack of trying."

Lykem clasped my shoulder. "Cillian has only slept and ate when he's been forced to. Even then, it hasn't been enough. He's spent hours scouring our realm for your daughter as have several others including myself."

They all seemed to ignore him, so I repeated much of the same.

"How is it that you can't find a single wolf amongst the dragons?" Roman asked, being held back by Cait and still seething.

"Our world isn't like yours," I said. "We have magic, but it's not something we can track. Someone has been attacking our realm for months now, and I believe that's who took Dawsyn, but I don't know why. What I do know is that I won't stop until I've found her."

"Yet, you're not looking for her now," Beatrix stated.

"Only because he knew her family deserved an update," Lykem interjected again.

Cait bowed her head once in my direction. "We appreciate that. Now, tell us how we can help."

"There isn't—" I started to speak, but Roman cut me off.

"Don't tell me there isn't anything we can do for our own daughter," he snapped. "You have no idea what we're capable of."

I held my hands up in defense. "I have no doubt that you're each a force to be reckoned with, and I would love the help, but I can't get you into my realm. Only those with dragon energy can get in."

"Yet, that's where my daughter is," he pointed out, forcing me to take the conversation in a direction I was hoping to avoid.

"I believe the person that took your daughter forced her to become his mate," I said, the words tasting like acid on my tongue and making my stomach churn.

"There's no other way they could have gotten her in?"

Cait asked, an ache in her tone that only a mother could have for their daughter in this situation.

I shook my head. "The connection I felt to her—one very strong—is gone. That would have only happened one way."

"Unless she figured out how to reject you," Roman said. "River told us that Dawsyn wasn't sure she wanted you."

No, she hadn't been, but I knew better. Dawsyn didn't do this because it was what she wanted.

"She wouldn't have disappeared like this and rejected him," Cait said. "And she would have needed a witch to help her. Something she shouldn't have known about."

All eyes went to Beatrix.

"Well, I didn't tell her," she said. "I didn't even tell the two of you when you wanted to know."

Lykem stepped forward. "If I can get the portal to allow others through, would you come help us?"

Roman answered with a resounding "yes" before Lykem had even finished speaking.

"That would be appreciated," Cait said as well.

Beatrix was the only one who didn't respond, but after our previous interactions, that didn't surprise me.

"Only two of our elders still live," Lykem said. "I will speak with them as soon as we return and see what can be done."

"How many have you lost?" Cait asked.

My friend's eyes cast down, and his voice lowered. "Too many."

"We need to get back," I said. "I have no way to communicate with you while I'm in Drago. We don't have cell phones there and never needed to figure out a way to communicate outside of our realm. But I do promise to come back just as soon as I have any news or in three more days, whichever comes first."

"It better be with news sooner than that," Roman grumbled, and I hoped like hell I could make that happen.

"Do you need anything from us?" Cait asked, and I glanced at Beatrix.

"Have you been able to acquire the items for the spell?"

There was a spark of something I didn't understand in her eyes until she began to speak. "Of course I have, but you won't get a single thing from me until my granddaughter is returned safely."

"What if the spell could help me get her back?" I asked.

"That spell would kill her if she wasn't prepared for it," Beatrix said pointedly. "Find her, bring her back, get the spell. End of discussion."

The witch turned her back on me and walked several steps away before she began opening a portal to somewhere with bright sunshine and a large grassy area.

Cait left Roman's side and reached for my hand, squeezing it forcefully. "Bring me back my daughter, Cillian."

"I will," I promised, and hoped like hell I wasn't lying.

Chapter Eight

DAWSYN

As long as we weren't losing count, I'd been gone for seven days. Every day had been different, and I never knew what to expect, but that didn't matter any longer. I was getting the hell out of this cage.

Earlier that morning, I was brought a bucket of clean water, a towel, and a white dress by The Psycho with strict instructions to get clean or else.

I wanted to laugh at her "or else" because she didn't frighten me, but I'd refrained, shrinking my body back.

I wanted them to think I was afraid in hopes that their guard would be lowered once I put my plan into action.

We can beat them regardless, my wolf said.

While I knew that, I wasn't opposed to anything I could do to make things easier.

Are you sure you're going to be okay? I asked her.

The main part of our plan involved me shifting and her running full speed out of there. She hadn't run for over a week, which could have had adverse effects.

I'll be more than fine, she replied.

I had no choice but to trust her.

While we waited for either Knox or Estelle to return, I took advantage of the things I'd been given and used the bucket to clean up. Though, I didn't leave my clothes off. I put them back on and put the white cotton dress over my jeans and t-shirt.

Part of my ruse was to keep my head down, step forward once the door was fully open, then shift. My wolf would then ram her head into whoever was standing in our path to freedom and we'd travel out the way we'd come in.

It was a plan with few steps, but there was so much that could go wrong. I wasn't going to forget that until we were far away from this fucking forest.

Several hours later, what I assumed to be early evening, the shield around my cell finally broke and the door opened.

I stayed huddled in the corner of the mattress with the dress pulled over my knees, hiding my other clothes, and peeked up through my lashes.

The relief I felt at seeing Estelle there, holding a light at her side, instead of Knox, was huge. I had enough motivation that I felt like I could have beaten Knox, but this just made things easier.

"Let's go," she grumbled. "Knox requires your presence."

Staying in the shadows as much as I could, I carefully slid off the bed and backed against the wall. "I don't want to go."

She raised a hand and stepped toward me, just far enough out of the way of the door like I'd hoped.

Now, I said to my wolf, and she pushed forward with a ferocity unlike I'd ever experienced from her.

Within the blink of an eye, we'd shifted, and there was a faint glow inside the room. Estelle paused, narrowly missing a claw to the face, but couldn't get out of the way before we slammed into her, our head driving into her stomach and knocking her against the opposite wall.

Her limp body was only in our peripherals for the briefest of seconds before we were barreling down the walkway between cells.

I felt bad for Darius—the only other person I knew to be down here—but I had to save myself before I could save anyone else.

Claws dug into the dirt surface, propelling us forward faster as I recalled the way we'd come before. Though, the counting of steps was no longer helpful considering I wasn't the one taking them.

I know where I'm going, my wolf said, turning sharply down another hallway.

We saw no one else for much longer than I expected, but there was a roar that echoed behind us that I had no problem hearing.

Faster, I urged.

We still didn't know if we were going to be able to open the door. Knox had said he was the only one that could open it when we arrived, but I had a small hope that people could leave of their own accord.

I would have liked to find that out ahead of time, but

the opportunity had never come. Trial by fire would have to be good enough.

"Dawsyn!" Knox screamed from somewhere too close behind me.

We're almost there, my wolf assured me as we continued to run.

There were two guards in front of us. Two men who weren't moving out of the way. I didn't know if they deserved to die or not, but we were left with very few choices when we got to them.

One swiped clawed hands at our front flank and the other grabbed onto our throat, squeezing hard.

Our saving grace was that none of these tunnels were big enough for them to fully shift, but that didn't mean these dragon shifters weren't tapping into their beasts' strength.

We kicked our hind legs out, pushing back one attacker and forcing him to release our throat. Without overthinking, my wolf's teeth ripped into the next guy's throat, tearing it out in one go.

The other one got back up, and we charged forward, cutting into his stomach with our claws and ramming him into the wall hard enough to knock him out.

If someone helped him soon enough, he might live, but that wasn't my concern at the moment.

Knox's bellows were too close for comfort, and the door was still too far away.

We're going to make it, my wolf vowed, and I did my best to keep her optimism at the forefront of my thoughts.

Two turns later and the stairs to the exit were right there in front of us. Just when we turned to go up, Knox's fist rammed into our side, knocking the air from our lungs.

Fuck, that hurts.

While I was stuck processing the pain, my wolf was still in defensive mode. She whipped our body around and bared her teeth at Knox, who merely laughed at us.

"Oh, Little Wolf," he cooed. "You're not leaving here until I'm done with you."

He reached forward, grabbing onto our front leg, and my wolf didn't hesitate in biting the shit out of his arm.

We have to hurt him enough that we'll have time to shift and me to open the door, I reminded my wolf.

She was powerful in her own right, but no matter how strong she was, that didn't change the fact she didn't have opposable thumbs.

Her responding snarl was enough confirmation that she hadn't forgotten the most important part of the plan.

Knox grabbed us again, but we were ready with claws and teeth. At least, we were until he sent a current of burning electricity through us.

My wolf's howl was soul piercing, and whatever ability Knox had was making our body cease to move any longer.

"I think I'll put a muzzle on you now. Maybe even a collar with my name on it to remind you that you're my bitch," Knox said as he grabbed us by the scruff. "You're coming with me and not leaving my sight again."

We couldn't hold back the whimper as he forced our body across the open area, further away from the door that led to our freedom.

Fuck. We'd been so close. I didn't know what I was going to do if Knox tried to force himself on me or touch me in any way other than he already had. The thought of it made my body vibrate with fury and disgust.

We have to get out of here, I said to my wolf. Not that she didn't already know that.

Her awareness wasn't all there, which I was thankful for when Knox threw us into a wall next to one of the other tunnels. "If you run again, the pain you're feeling now will seem like child's play."

I wanted to scream "fuck you" in his smug face, but there was little to no strength left in me. With my wolf fading out, I was resigned to accept that I was stuck here a little longer, but that didn't mean we wouldn't try again.

He zapped us one more time, but this one didn't pack as much heat. "Now, get up and walk. I'm not carrying you back to my room."

This jolt somehow had the opposite effect as the previous one. My wolf's consciousness returned with vigor, and her responding snarl shocked not only me but Knox.

"I will hurt you, Little Wolf," he warned, holding his hand out with a red glow at the center of his palm.

What are you doing? I asked my wolf, but she didn't answer me. At least, not with words.

A soft glow began to grow around us, and she charged forward again. Knox grabbed on to her, but the blinding agony he caused before was nothing more than a mere tickle.

How are you doing that? I asked, but still didn't get a reply from my wolf.

She remained focused on Knox, trying to tear her teeth into his neck, but he did a partial shift. His scales were protecting him, and we didn't have time to figure out how to end him. It was more important to get away at this point.

We leapt over him, kicking his head as we raced back toward the stairs. He seemed dazed from whatever the glow around us had been from, and I didn't waste a second questioning it.

I shifted back to my human form and held my breath as I finished running up the stairs and pressed a palm over the wooden door, then used my other hand to twist the handle. Energy moved through the solid surface, but it wouldn't push open.

I glanced back and Knox was starting to get back up. Panic began to set in, and I shoved harder at the door, squeezing the handle until the metal started to bend under my hold.

"Open the fuck up," I hissed.

One last glance back showed Knox was on his hands and knees, his eyes on me and filled with unfiltered wrath.

Finally, the door opened and I raced through it, sucking in the fresh air, but not for long.

My wolf pushed forward again, and we shifted mid-run as Knox came chasing us out of the door. Only, he stopped about ten feet into the forest. When we checked behind us, he was just standing there with his arms crossed.

Why isn't he chasing us? I asked, wondering if we'd just done exactly what he hoped.

Not that I'd really expected an answer, but my wolf still didn't reply.

Are you okay? I asked this time. *What was that back there?*

Her body shuddered but powered forward. *Moon Goddess energy.*

What? Like Luna Marked?

She was quiet a beat longer. *Yes and no.*

What the fuck does that mean? I demanded.

It means we have a similar energy as your mother, but we're not like her.

I'd fucking known it.

All my life, I'd wondered if there was something more deep down inside me. Thank the Moon Goddess I'd been right. She'd shown up for us just in time.

Chapter Nine

CILLIAN

Every day, I was drawn to the dark forest. Yet every day, I found nothing that got me closer to finding Dawsyn.

Knowing she was here, but not knowing exactly where or how to reach her was driving me and my dragon to insanity. It didn't matter that our bond with Dawsyn had been broken. We needed *her*.

I didn't need the fates to tell me she was who I wanted. She was the person who challenged me. The one who knew her value, but still held the wellbeing of others above herself. Someone I would die to let live.

It didn't matter that I'd only known her for a few weeks. I knew Dawsyn's worth just as much as she did, and she was worth everything.

As I flew over the forest for the tenth time that day, I tried to focus on the strength I knew my mate held within her. She was a fighter. Whatever was happening to her, she wouldn't give up trying to get free.

My dragon soared over the trees, his wings stretched

wide and the dimming sun reflecting off his scales, making them seem more golden than earthy. He was content being home—the lightning power inside us settled for the time being. The only thing that could make this better was having Dawsyn.

Finding my grandmother would also help. I'd not only been looking for my mate, but also wondering where Nannio had escaped to. She'd never made it to the caves. Not one person I'd asked had seen her or known where she might have gone.

I hated to think she'd met the same fate as my uncles, but I wasn't sure what other options there could be. Focusing on Dawsyn had helped me ignore the grief of losing two of the three family members I had left, but I knew the day would come when I couldn't hold everything in.

For the time being, I stayed busy searching for my mate.

Lykem's red dragon flew toward us, coming in fast before turning his wings, gliding over and above me, then settling in next to us.

Any signs? he asked telepathically. I wished that worked outside of Drago with more than just my family, but at least we had that ability here, thanks to the energy of our realm.

Nothing new or different, I replied. *I don't like that the destruction has ceased.*

He chuckled. *Everyone else does. People want to go home.*

But that's likely what this psycho wants, I said. *For the few of us left to come out of the caves so he can pick us off one by one.*

Lykem stayed silent for a beat, then his dragon head

nodded. *Probably, but what is a life lived in fear? We have to do something.*

I knew searching for Dawsyn every day and night wasn't what was best for my people, but I couldn't give up on her yet.

We will. Soon, I promised.

At least they would. I had a feeling that if I didn't bring Dawsyn back with me tomorrow when I was supposed to check in with her parents, I was going to be a dead man.

It wasn't that I didn't think I could beat Roman in a fight, but I could never hurt Dawsyn's dad and expect her to forgive me. I'd rather die than live with that guilt.

Did you hear that? Lykem asked, turning his wings.

There was a rumble in the distance, coming from deep within the dark forest. *That* was something new.

I sped past him, wings flapping furiously.

Please, fucking let this be her.

The previous rumble didn't repeat again, but we were already zeroed in on where the sound had come from.

As we approached, there was a glow within the trees, moving faster than I could track through the thick foliage with my eyes, going in the opposite direction.

You go toward the noise, I said to Lykem. *I'm going to follow whatever that was.*

Are you sure we should split up?

I was already turned around before he'd even finished asking the question.

We don't have a choice.

Whatever was out there had to lead me to the answers I'd been searching for. Someone had escaped, and that meant Dawsyn could as well.

Though, as I caught up with the glow, my entire body filled with fire that powered me forward with an urgency I'd yet to experience.

My dragon nose-dived toward the trees, getting closer to the speeding...wolf. I could scent the wolf shifter, but they didn't smell like my Dawsyn. Though, that didn't stop my heart from beating wildly.

A howl cut through the air that quickly turned into a snarl as I got closer. She was running out of the trees and cut right to stay under the foliage. If it wasn't for the bright glow, I wouldn't have been able to track her, but I couldn't take my eyes off the powerful energy I was sensing.

Deciding the only way to get to this wolf was to get ahead of her, I flew past her, working my wings harder than ever before. My dragon form crashed through the branches a few moments later and landed just a few yards in front of the wolf shifter.

Only one look into her golden eyes and I knew this wasn't some supreme wolf that had been trapped down there with Dawsyn. This was my mate.

Her wolf stopped, chest heaving, then let out a sorrowful howl I couldn't understand.

I shifted immediately back to my human form and held my hands out. "It's okay, Dawsyn. I'm not going to hurt you. I want to take you home."

She whimpered some more, and the glow around her reddish-grey wolf began to die down. I hesitated to step forward. I wasn't sure where her head was at, and I didn't want to rush her, but damn it, I was dying inside to hold her again.

Her wolf laid down on the leaf-covered ground, and I

held my arm out, palm up and toward her. "I'm going to come closer."

She whimpered again, head down and eyes averted.

I didn't understand what I was sensing. Her wolf was putting off vibes of shame, but that made no sense. This wasn't who Dawsyn was. Not that I'd seen since knowing her, at least.

When I was within reaching distance, I lowered to one knee and lightly placed my hand on her head. The wolf shuddered and half whimpered while groaning.

"It's okay, Dawsyn," I promised. "Whatever happened, we'll work it out together."

Her head shook, and she jerked back from me.

"If you'd shift back, this would be a lot easier for me to understand," I said, then added, "but if you're not comfortable around me, then stay however you'd like. We really should get out of here, though."

Lykem still wasn't back from following whatever had caused that rumble. It could have been the dragon shifter I assumed was causing all the mayhem in Drago. Not being there for my friend in case he needed back-up wasn't sitting right with me, but Dawsyn needed me more.

Whatever had happened to her, she wasn't okay.

Her wolf finally stood up on four legs, then shimmered briefly before she transformed back to her human self.

My eyes roamed over her face, surprised to see she was clean and put together, but as I took in her clothes, I realized that wasn't exactly the case.

She was wearing a white dress over the jeans and t-shirt I'd last seen her in, and it was covered in red dirt and ripped in a few places, as if she'd been fighting in it.

I stepped closer, my fingers twitching to hold her. "Dawsyn."

As I said her name, all the desperation I'd been feeling since the bond had been taken away leaked through the single word.

Her eyes finally met mine and glossed over. I'd never seen my mate vulnerable, but when she leapt into my arms, tears falling down her cheeks and arms wrapped so tightly around me that I could hardly breathe, I knew something had broken her. Or someone. And they were going to die for doing this to her.

I rubbed my hands over her back as her arms and legs clung to me. "It's okay. I have you."

"I'm so sorry," she murmured into my neck. "I didn't have another choice."

Did she think I was mad about the bond breaking? I fucking hoped not.

"You have nothing to apologize for." I pushed her back until I could see her face again. "You're mine, Dawsyn. Bond or not, I'd never give up on you."

"Fuck," she hissed, then grabbed both of my cheeks and pressed her lips to mine.

I was tempted to devour her, but she was fragile and needed this control, so I let her have it.

She kissed me slowly at first, but never loosened her hold on my face or around my waist. I kept one hand on her neck and the other over her ass, pushing her closer to me.

Her tongue urged forward, and I opened for her, moaning into the kiss, needing her more than I ever had before.

Her hands moved to the back of my head, digging her

nails into my skin. The bite of pain was welcome until she tensed within my hold.

"What's wrong?" I asked softly.

"Someone's coming." The fear that emanated from the two words was like a knife to my chest.

I listened and sensed for what she already had and realized it was just Lykem.

"It's okay," I said. "He's friendly, but we should still go."

She clung tighter to me. "Go where?"

"For the moment, to the caves where the rest of the dragons are staying. Then, we'll get you back to Earth."

The tension in her shoulder loosened some, and she nodded. "Okay."

"How do you feel about riding a dragon?" I asked, trying and failing to hide my grin.

Her eyes finally sparked the way they had when I first met her. "Depends on the situation."

She might have been scared, but my mate was still strong.

I grabbed her hand and led her out of the forest. "Come on. We need to know if there's anything else to worry about right now."

The grimace on her face didn't make me feel better. "There's a lot we need to talk about."

"We'll get to that," I said. "Soon."

My thoughts got away from me, wondering about what could have happened to her, given she was forced to become someone else's mate...

I'd done my best not to let my thoughts go to those dark places. Instead, I'd focused on how capable I knew

Dawsyn was and known that she'd fight to keep herself safe.

Except, seeing her now, shaken to the core, I couldn't help but wonder if she'd been worse off than I'd let myself believe.

That caused rage to swirl deep inside my chest, expanding through the rest of my body, but this wasn't about me. It was about my mate. I had to keep my thoughts focused on Dawsyn and be thankful she was back with me.

I could plot murder as soon as I had her safely away from this fucking forest that had hidden her from me.

Chapter Ten

DAWSYN

I'd thought I was okay. Thought I'd come out of that whole situation like a badass with no issues, but the moment I realized I wasn't just an ordinary alpha wolf and then thought I was running for my life again from an attacking dragon, I'd lost it.

When I realized that it was Cillian following me and not Knox, I'd calmed considerably, but only for a moment. Once the true loss of the connection was right there in front of us, I couldn't ignore the sorrow that consumed my wolf.

She'd been mated to his dragon before. She knew his soul and yearned for the comfort that could only come from our bond. Yet, she'd never even had the chance to properly have it.

Knox had stolen that from us. Before we returned to a vengeful mindset, both my wolf and I gave into the grief of what was lost. We gave into the warmth that Cillian was offering and wept.

After being locked away, after not really knowing if I'd

get out of that underground bunker unscathed... Having our true mate hold us was everything.

His touch healed the parts of me that I'd shoved down while we'd been in that cell. The parts I couldn't risk coming to the surface without losing all of my will to fight.

As he held my hand and guided me out of the forest, the tension in my body began to slowly release. I forced myself to breathe deeply and remember that I was okay.

Different than before, but okay.

The glow around me was a problem for later, though. Cillian needed to know what I'd learned.

Before we could get to that, my eyes landed on a ginormous red dragon. A deep rich color that had shinier scales which reflected the dull sun above. Seeing this one made me wish that we'd slowed enough earlier to get a better look at Cillian's beast.

We'll get that time later, my wolf said, and I agreed. We had time now that we weren't certain we'd have before.

The dragon in front of us was ten-or-so feet tall before he began to shrink down. Within a few seconds, a man stood in his place with a wide smile on his face. His skin glowed with a light tan, making his short reddish-blond hair stand out.

He winked at me with his blue eyes, and he reached a hand toward me. "You must be Dawsyn. I'm Lykem."

"Like-em?" I pronounced the name slower, making sure I didn't insult him later by saying it wrong.

"Yep." Then, he leaned closer and lowered his voice. "But some of the ladies like to call me *Lick*-em as well. I'll answer to either."

I couldn't help but laugh at his lack of modesty.

Though, that didn't last long once Cillian's arm wrapped around my shoulders and his chest rumbled.

Apparently, he didn't need the bond to be possessive. And that was perfectly okay with me.

Just the mere thought of our lost connection had me rubbing my chest where I used to feel the pull toward him.

"Are you okay?" Cillian asked quietly.

I nodded. "Where do we go now?"

He and Lykem shared a look, and the latter shook his head. "I didn't see anyone. Wherever they'd come from, they disappeared again before I got there."

"I know where he went," I said.

Both of them stared down at me, equal amounts of curiosity pouring from them, but it was Cillian who spoke first. "Let's get back to the caves before we have that discussion. We don't know how safe it is out here."

Lykem stepped away and began to shift back to his dragon form, then Cillian turned to me. "You don't have to ride on my back if you'd rather run as your wolf. I can fly low and stay close to you."

While being high up in the air didn't sound all that appealing to me or my wolf, I had little desire to separate from my mate now that I'd found him again.

"Go ahead and shift," I said casually. "Is there anywhere I shouldn't sit?"

Lykem's dragon had small spikes up his neck, and I'd rather not be too close to one of those if Cillian had them as well.

"Anywhere you feel safe is perfect," Cillian answered, then pulled me in for a quick kiss before he moved away to shift.

My eyes stayed fixed on his body, wanting to see every moment of his transformation. The air around him began to flicker with opaque energy, and unfiltered power radiated from his skin. He kept his stare on me until the last second, then closed his eyes.

Quicker than I could track, his body shifted and elongated, growing ten times its previous size and becoming a dragon even larger than Lykem's.

Cillian's back had to be close to fifteen feet from the ground, and as he stretched his wings, I could see those were nearly as wide as he was tall. His tail flicked out behind him with three spikes at the end that I assumed were rather deadly in certain situations.

His scales reminded me of rocks. Stone-like until the sun hit them, making them seem more golden. There were also several splashes of blue that stood out against the earthy color.

Eyeing the rest of his body so I could figure out the best way to climb onto his back, I noticed small spikes along his neck that became larger at the top of his head, but not as big as the ones on his tail.

Staying at the center of his back where my feet could rest on his wings was probably ideal, but before I jumped on, I walked toward him and rubbed my hands over his chest.

The scales were smoother than I'd assumed, more polished and less...snakelike. Though, I wouldn't be telling him that was what I'd expected.

His body rumbled beneath my touch, and he lowered his head. I moved my touch to his face, and his eyes fluttered closed.

"You're magnificent," I whispered to his dragon, eliciting another echoing rumble.

He appreciates your...appreciation, my wolf said, making my entire body stiffen.

You can talk to his dragon? I'd known that fated wolves could talk to each other, but I didn't think that same notion applied to those not created by the Moon Goddess.

We've been mated before, she reminded me. *I still have a connection to him even though you don't.*

That made me mildly jealous, but more than that, after everything we'd been through this last week, I was thankful she had that with him.

I gave his face one more gentle rub, then moved over to where his front leg was beneath his wing. Reaching up, I grabbed the edge of his left wing and stepped up onto his leg, pulling myself up.

He stayed perfectly still, and the rest was easier than I expected. Within a few seconds, I was seated in the middle of his back, the tips of my toes resting on his wings and my hands holding onto the slight humps down his spine.

It wasn't the most comfortable spot in the world, but I felt safe there.

He flapped his wings and pushed into the sky. As soon as we were off the ground, I leaned forward, pressing my stomach against his back and wrapping my arms around him.

This position wasn't any safer—it was probably worse, given I didn't have much to grasp onto around his sides—but as the wind came at me, lower just felt better.

Calm down. We're fine, my wolf said.

How the hell do you know that?

Because if we fall off, they'll catch us.

I gaped. That's *supposed to make me feel better?*

That's up to you.

If I could choke her, some days, I was certain that I would.

As much as I wanted to see Cillian's world from this vantage point, I couldn't keep my eyes open. My stomach churned every time I tried to peek.

I didn't think you were afraid of heights, my wolf chided.

This is not a heights thing. Not even fucking close.

This was like the world's worst roller coaster.

I sensed her amusement but did my best to ignore her, especially when Cillian's dragon dipped quickly toward the ground and the previous day's dinner tried to come back up.

Mother shittery shit.

The landing was smooth, at least, and I took a steadying breath before getting off his back. I didn't want Cillian to know that I never wanted to do that again.

Once I felt solid enough, I jumped to the ground, stepping away from his dragon so he could shift back.

Before I could turn around to watch, his arms were already circling around my back and hugging me from behind. "How was that?"

"Fun," I answered, glad I wasn't looking right at him.

Liar, my wolf goaded.

Shut it, wolf.

"We'll go out again for a longer ride once it's safe," he promised, and I selfishly hoped that it was never safe. I was officially a terrible person.

"Come on, lovebirds," Lykem called from the trees. "We need to update the others."

I tensed, knowing that I not only had to tell Cillian that he had a brother, but also that his Nannio was a psychotic traitor.

It was a conversation I wasn't looking forward to.

Cillian glanced back at his friend. "I need to talk with Dawsyn first. We'll be there shortly."

Lykem nodded once, then disappeared into the side of a snowy mountain.

"Where's he going?" I asked.

"Inside the caves of that mountain," Cillian answered. "It's where those who are left have been living for the last few weeks." His eyes searched my face. "If you don't want to talk about what happened yet, you don't have to."

I knew that, which was why I needed to. He deserved to know what I did as soon as possible.

"It's okay, but we should probably sit." It was colder toward the mountain, so I moved in the direction I sensed the heat that had been sweltering near the town.

We walked nearly a minute and found a flat enough rock. I sat on the top and turned to face him. My heart yearned to feel the bond, searched for the tether that was no longer there.

Cillian grabbed my hands and squeezed. "Whatever happened, we'll figure out a way to make it right."

I decided to start with the easier subject. "I broke our bond. I mated with another dragon shifter."

His thumb rubbed over my palm. "I know. To save River."

"He's okay, right?" If I'd done all that for nothing, I was going to lose my shit.

He nodded. "As far as I know, yes. Justine was with him, and he'd texted me while I was still looking for you, warning me about your family."

My hand covered my mouth. "Oh hell. My parents."

"Are furious and we'll need to see them tomorrow," he said. "Beatrix was also with them when I went back to Earth to let everyone know that I hadn't found you yet. She has everything we need for the spell. She also said she knew how to break a bond. So, whoever you had to bond with to get into Drago, she can remove the connection."

I shuddered at the memory of Knox placing one of his scales in the cut on my hand. I didn't think anything had ever felt more terrible.

"We'll have her do that first thing," I said. "I would have never chosen him if I'd had another choice. I meant what I said before you left, Cillian."

His smile was soft and soothed some of my worries. "I know. It's the only reason I stayed somewhat sane while you were gone. I knew you needed me still." He paused, his gaze briefly moving to our combined hands. "Besides the bond, he didn't force you to do anything you didn't want to, right?"

I was shaking my head before he finished asking. "My wolf would have bit his dick off."

He finally laughed, and the sound filled my chest with warmth. At least until he asked his next question.

"Who took you?"

This was my opening. He wasn't furious with me for

tying myself to someone else as I thought he had every right to be. I needed to tell him who it was.

"About that," I said, looking away from him and out toward the barren land. "The person who took me...said he's your brother."

Cillian's body stiffened next to me, and I finally looked back over at him. His eyes pinched at the sides, and there was a tic in his left cheek that normally wasn't there.

"He was lying," he said stiffly.

Oh, how I wish I could let him believe that.

"I don't know if you share the same parents or just one, but I don't think he was lying."

"Why?" he practically growled.

"Because I saw someone else there," I answered. "Someone that I think you're also related to."

He closed his eyes briefly, and when he reopened them, the amount of rage he had building inside seemed to lessen.

"Whatever you say," he said, "I won't blame you, and I know this isn't your fault. I can handle whatever you learned."

I knew he could. That wasn't why I didn't want to tell him. I just didn't want to hurt him.

"Your grandmother was there," I said. "She brought me food most days. Spoke with Knox—your, uh, brother—in a way that confirmed he was related to her."

His face paled. "She's working with him?"

"I think so. It doesn't seem like the best working relationship, and he called her Estelle instead of Nannio like you do, but there was no doubt that she was there willingly."

Scales appeared on his arms as he released the hold that

he had on my hands, fisting his fingers and tightening his jaw. "You're sure?"

I nodded once.

"I'd thought she was dead." His voice was void of emotion. "That would have been better."

Chapter Eleven

CILLIAN

My Nannio, a traitor? If I'd heard it from anyone else, I would have had a much harder time believing them, but Dawsyn had no reason to lie to me. She had no agenda here, no ties to this world besides me.

The thoughts racing through my mind weren't good. Not for me or anyone. How long had Estelle—as I'd now call her—been working with this Knox person? Could *he* really be my brother? How and when would he have been born?

What was the purpose of sending me to Mystics Academy to find something to stop Knox if she was working with him? Did she expect me to find nothing and fail? Was the trip just to get me out of the way?

The potential answers to those questions infuriated me to no end and had more scales pushing forcefully through my skin. I tried to calm my rage, but nothing I could think about in that moment was helping.

All I could sense was the betrayal. Had Knox killed my uncles? What vendetta could he possibly have against our family and realm that would bring him to this kind of destruction?

Sure, if he really was my brother and one or both of my parents had abandoned him at some point, I could understand being vengeful, but bringing down an entire realm? There had to be more to this than what I was attempting to piece together.

"Did you hear any of their conversations?" I asked Dawsyn. "Did they say anything about why they were doing this?"

She reached for me, running the backs of her fingers over my arm that was still covered in scales. "Are you sure you want to keep talking about this right now?"

"We don't have a lot of time," I said. "People want to go back to their homes. We only have so much food."

She nodded toward the scales. "Does that hurt when you do that?"

"It's...uncomfortable, but don't change the subject."

Her huff of annoyance was endearing. "Fine." She began to rattle off everything that had happened since the moment she was taken. How Knox had shown up and she'd almost gotten away, but then he'd mentioned River and shown her a photo of him beaten and tied to a chair. Told her that if she didn't choose to be his mate, then she'd be a murderer.

A fucking low blow that wouldn't have been true even if River had died, but knowing what I knew about Dawsyn, she would have taken those words to heart.

Then there was the warlock that had tried to keep his identity hidden, but Dawsyn saw a tattoo that she intended to tell Beatrix about. That was my mate's vendetta, and I'd happily support her in getting back at that warlock for hurting her best friend.

By the time she got to the part about the hidden door in the forest, my body was shaking. The only thing that kept me from snapping was the fact that Knox hadn't actually touched her.

Though, keeping her sealed in a dark cell wasn't how I suspected someone would treat their mate, even a forced one. That made me even more confused about Knox's reasons for all this destruction.

"There was one other person that I heard them talking to in the cells," she said. "Knox wanted some sort of payment from him, but the man had refused."

Could have been another dragon with powerful scales. They existed much like mine. If used with certain energies, they could create electricity with the force of a lightning bolt. I hadn't warned Beatrix about that. If she wanted to play with things she didn't understand, she could learn the hard way.

"We have to go back for him," she added. "The man—Darius. I left him behind, but I made a promise to myself that I'd go back."

My entire body froze, and my voice strained. "Darius? You're sure that's his name?"

Her eyes creased at the sides, likely confused by my strong reaction. "Yeah. Knox was beating the shit out of him, and Estelle told him to stop. It sounded like they were using him for something important, but he was done being used and ready to die."

I closed my eyes briefly and thought about every dragon I'd met over the years. Not just the thousands who had lived right here, but even those who lived further out in the mountains.

There had only ever been one Darius, and I hadn't seen him since I was twelve years old.

"My father's name was Darius," I said. "You're absolutely certain that was the name they used?"

Of course, I hadn't met every dragon in Drago, but given how tightly wound into this situation my family was... It couldn't be a coincidence.

Dawsyn's face paled. "I think it's him. Knox said something." She bit the inside of her cheek. "Shit. What was it?"

I waited as patiently as I could while she thought back. Her fingers pressed over her temples and then she jerked her head up. "'It will be your blood I come for next.' That's what he said to Estelle. Is she your dad's mom?"

I nodded, both of us putting the pieces together. Estelle had never been forthcoming about her talents. She preferred to act out and let people think she was crazy, but I'd always assumed it was a façade to hide her true power. Whatever it was...Knox thought he could use it as well.

But my father. His was fire. The fireballs being launched over the town were beginning to make more sense.

Fuck. I thought I'd feel better knowing more about the person we'd been trying to find for months. Instead, all I felt was unfiltered ire and hurt.

Family was important to most dragons. We stuck together, always, but somewhere along the way, one of my parents left a son behind. Now he was trying to take everything from me.

That wasn't going to fucking work for me.

Dawsyn grabbed my face with both hands. "Hey. Look at me. You're okay. Whatever he's done can't be changed, but we'll stop him from hurting anyone else."

I couldn't speak. The rage was too tightly wound inside me, but somehow, even without the bond, Dawsyn knew this.

She stood from the rock, then glanced down at herself with a sneer. "This needs to fucking go."

I hadn't put too much thought into why she'd been wearing a dress over her jeans and shirt, but as she ripped the fabric from her body, I had a feeling it was something she'd been forced to wear.

Once the scraps of material dropped to the ground, she put her hands back on my face and smiled. "Better."

Her fingers stroked over my rough skin, thanks to the dragon inside dying to come out and destroy every inch of the dark forest.

Her legs inched closer until she could straddle my lap, locking her ankles around my back.

As her hands moved from my face to the back of my head, every nerve in my body ignited. I gripped her hips, holding tightly and anchoring her to me. "Dawsyn, you don't need to calm me down this way."

"Who said this was for you?" she snarked. "I just spent a week in a dank cell, isolated and waiting for bad shit to happen to me. Maybe it's me who needs you."

She was lying. We both knew it. But I didn't stop her when she pressed her lips to the tip of my nose, my forehead, both cheeks, and then my mouth.

I gently kissed her back, letting her distract the rage

inside me. With every touch, my muscles relaxed but my heart still raced—only for very different reasons.

"Your scales are gone," she whispered against my ear before scraping her teeth along the edge.

A shiver shot through me and straight to my balls. "They won't be for long if you keep that up."

Her hips rolled over my lap, pressing her center firmly over my hardening cock. "What about this?"

"You're a tease." I growled.

She jerked back, nails digging into my shoulders and her eyes darkening. "Make no mistake, Cillian. I want you. This isn't a ploy to calm you down. I've missed every aggravating moment with you. Missed the way you say my name and how it felt to kiss you for the first time." She kissed me softer. "How you make my heart race."

I'd worried things with us would be different, thanks to the tie she now had to Knox, but hearing her say those words, feeling how true each of them was... It was everything I didn't know I needed.

"I missed you so fucking much, Dawsyn," I murmured, pressing my forehead to hers. "Almost to the point of insanity."

She raised my chin with two fingers and grinned. "Show me."

That I could do.

My palm pressed against her spine, pushing her closer to me, and my other hand angled her jaw just before my lips captured hers.

She opened for me before my tongue had even slid forward. Her hips ground forward, and I moved to grip the back of her head.

The heat of her body seeped into me, consuming every inch of my soul and more. All I could feel were her hips moving above me and her nails cutting through my shirt. Every thought I'd had before this moment was gone. All that was left was Dawsyn.

My mate. No matter what happened next.

Her teeth scraped over my lower lip, and she pressed her forehead against mine, chest heaving nearly as much as mine was.

"I'm assuming there are no bedrooms in that cave back there," she said softly, but I could hear the smile in her words.

"Not exactly. Unless you count sheets as walls and blankets as mattresses." I hadn't thought that was a problem for me before, but having Dawsyn back in my arms, I couldn't wait to truly have her all to myself.

She kissed me again, then slipped a hand between us, her fingers rubbing over my erection through my jeans. "We're going to have to do something about that."

"There are a lot of things we need to do something about, but not out here," I said with regret. I wanted her in this moment, but more than that, I didn't want anyone else to see more of my mate than they should be allowed.

She wiggled over my lap, a wicked grin on her perfect face. "Are you sure? I can be quiet."

She was fucking killing me. "Even if that's true, Lykem would have already told people we found you, and I doubt they'll give us enough time for me to enjoy you like I want to and like you deserve."

"And people say chivalry is dead." She tsked. "We'll make time soon, though. Really fucking soon."

My dragon swirled inside me. The need to claim her was damn near overwhelming, but until the bond she had to...Knox was broken, that wasn't going to be possible.

"You'll need to convince your grandmother to help us first," I said, gripping her chin between my fingers. "I want you mine in every way, Dawsyn Chase."

"And you'll have me," she promised, kissing me once more.

I held on tightly to her, hoping like hell that was true.

Chapter Twelve

DAWSYN

Between my wolf's wants and my own hormones, I'd have fucked Cillian right on that rock with no regrets. At least, not at that moment.

As much as I hated to admit it, he was right to tell me no. He wasn't just some guy I was letting off steam with. He was the only mate I should have ever had. I'd wasted time thinking I needed to be on my own, and now I was paying for that.

Seeing how hurt he'd been over what I'd told him nearly killed me. The pain he'd easily turned into rage was palpable. I'd practically tasted the fire inside him.

Though, there was a deeper part of him that I could sense had been irrevocably changed by everything he'd had to endure this last week—losing our bond, learning he had a brother, his grandmother was a traitor, and his father was alive...

I had a feeling he wouldn't quite be himself for a while, and understandably so, but I wasn't going anywhere. I'd be the strength he needed right now, bond or not. We were in this together.

At least I'd been able to ease the worst of it with my version of a distraction. Even if we hadn't really gotten to *do* anything. Though, if we'd continued much longer, I would have happily dry-humped him into an orgasm. That was how desperately I'd missed and needed him.

Admitting it now was freeing. It felt odd to think that needing someone so much could release me, but it was the truth. I'd fought it but wouldn't any longer.

I slid off his lap and stood up, reaching a hand to him. "What now?"

His fingers easily slipped between mine and tugged me toward his chest. "Now, I think thoughts about baby scapese, so that Lykem doesn't get the joy of commenting on my current situation."

"First, I told you I'd have remedied that," I teased. "Secondly, what the hell are baby scapese?"

His head jerked slightly back. "You don't have those on Earth?"

"Not that I'm aware of."

He seemed overly confused by that statement. "They're white fluffy things about the size of a watermelon. Big floppy ears and they jump around a lot. No tail, just a little ball of fur."

I gaped at him. "Do you mean a bunny? Or rabbit?"

"What is that?"

I slapped my hand to my forehead. And here I'd thought our worlds were practically parallel.

"I'm rather positive it's your version of a scapese," I

answered. "Now, I feel like I should question everything." I pointed behind me. "Is that a rock?"

"Yes," he deadpanned, clearly not as shocked by this revelation as I was. "I did survive in your realm for four weeks without not knowing the proper name of something. I think this could be a one-off."

I hummed. "We'll see."

He led us toward the cave entrance, and I was surprised by how dark it was. "People have been living in here?"

"Yes, but further back," he said. "There's another opening on the other side. They set up in the middle so they could escape from either end if there was an attack on the mountain."

Smart dragons. Given what I'd seen of their town, I was surprised there hadn't been an ambush out here yet.

"How many people are here?" I asked.

He grimaced. "Only a couple hundred. There used to be several thousand that lived in the village you saw back there."

My chest ached for their people. So many lives pointlessly lost. There'd been no purpose in the attacks. At least, not that I could see. I almost wished I'd had more time with Knox so I could have figured out why he was doing these things, but at the same time, I was grateful he'd wanted little to do with me until the end.

Cillian threaded his fingers through mine and led the way inside the cave. My vision adjusted within seconds, thanks to the ambient light. While it wasn't bright, I could see well enough. Though, there wasn't much to see at first besides a dirt path and slate grey rock walls.

"What can you do?" I asked him, thinking about how I'd had no idea what he was capable of as a dragon shifter.

"Huh?"

"Can you breathe fire? See in the dark? Scent things from long distances? Run super fast?"

"Oh," he replied. "Well, I can see inside these caves just as clearly as if we were outside still, but if I was somewhere like you'd described the cell, I probably wouldn't be able to. I run faster than a human, but not like a vampire. Fire is touchy. Every dragon can produce enough heat to make smoke and embers, but we don't necessarily breathe it like the fables would have you believe. Though, there are some dragons who can create fire with their dragon energy like I can with lightning."

I jerked him to a stop. "I'm sorry, what? Lightning?"

He grimaced. "I thought I told you about that."

"Um, nope. Pretty sure I would have remembered that." I was tempted to ask him to show me, but that probably wasn't a good idea in such a confined space.

"What about you?" he asked. "I've never seen a glowing wolf before."

He tried to guide us forward again, but I couldn't move. Somehow, with all the fear and adrenaline and hurt pumping through my veins, I'd completely forgotten that my wolf had become something entirely new as we'd run for our lives.

Cillian must have sensed the shift in my mood, because in the next second, his hands were cupping my face and his eyes were level with mine. "What's wrong?"

"I've never done that before today," I admitted. "I'd

always wondered if I had inherited powers from my mother, but nobody could tell me if it was even possible."

"Powers? What can your mother do?"

"She's Luna Marked," I said, as if that should make sense to him. "It's a longer story than we should get into right now, but her wolf is stronger than nearly any other. At least when she's in danger. The power doesn't seem to always stay with her."

"And the glow around you earlier is something she can also do?" he asked hesitantly.

I shrugged. "Yes and no. Her wolf is sometimes this stunning purple color, but it was less the glow of earlier than the rush of energy I'd felt."

My wolf had been rather quiet on the subject, but since I'd been so distracted with Cillian, I assumed she'd been distracted by his dragon as well.

We need to update the dragons before we worry about us, she finally said.

At least she wasn't completely ignoring me in favor of our mate.

Fair enough, I said to her then nudged Cillian forward. "I'm good. I promise. It was just a surprise and I'll need to talk to my mom about it tomorrow when we see them."

Thankfully, he dropped the subject, and we continued through the narrow path until it opened up into a smaller room with more pathways.

Lykem was standing there with another man about his height. Both of them were grinning. "Penn fixed the portal," Lykem said.

I tilted my head and looked at Cillian. "What was wrong with it?"

"Technically, nothing," he answered. "But we told your family that we'd try to figure out a way to get them into Drago without having to be bonded to a dragon. Though, they don't really have a reason to come here now."

"They absolutely do," I said. "The fight here is far from over. You're going to need help, and they can do that."

"I can't ask your family to fight for our people," he replied just as Lykem said, "That's the best idea anyone has had yet."

The two friends stared each other down, and the other dragon approached me. He looked about the same age as Lykem and Cillian, somewhere in their twenties. He had light-brown hair that was shaved short at the sides and green eyes that seemed to shimmer with a layer of blue under the flickering light of the fire torches on the walls around us.

"I'm Penn." He reached a hand to me. "You must be Dawsyn."

"Yep. Nice to meet you." My stare held his, but he quickly looked away and released my hand as Cillian towered over me from behind.

"Who knows that the portal has been opened to more than dragons?" Cillian asked.

"I only just told Lykem," Penn answered.

"Keep it that way," Cillian said gruffly. "We won't be bringing anyone else here unless we have to, and we don't need others thinking they can come and go as they please with new guests until we sort this mess out."

Mentioning others had me second-guessing the portal being open at all. "Knox was working with a warlock. I don't know what his plans are, but if he figures out that he can bring others here, you might have an even bigger fight on your hands."

Cillian glared at Lykem. "Do you understand now?"

The other dragon turned to Penn. "Can you put a blocker over it that only we can open and close?"

"Possibly. It was a complicated spell to undo," he answered. "I'll need to head back out there to try a few things."

"Go with him," Cillian said to Lykem. "We don't know how quickly there might be another attack now that we have Dawsyn. Nobody should be going out alone."

It was interesting to see the dynamic here. Not once had Cillian given me the idea that he was any sort of leader, but Lykem nodded without further question and the two dragons headed toward a different tunnel than we'd come from.

"What now?" I asked him once we were alone.

"Now, I introduce you to a few more dragons and we tell them what you learned while you were locked up." His shoulders tensed and jaw twitched.

"We don't have to right now," I said. "Everything I learned directly affects you and your family. That can't be easy."

"Not much about life is easy. Might as well get it over with."

This sullen version of Cillian wasn't something I was used to. The events of the past week were hurting him more than he was letting on.

I wanted to help ease his pain, but this was on Cillian to process. I couldn't force him to do something he wasn't ready for yet.

He lowered his head and rubbed his hands over my arms. "I wish we could have met under different circumstances."

"I'm not going to lie or pretend I don't agree with that, but—" I pressed my lips to his. "—maybe this was exactly what we both needed."

I didn't know all of Cillian's wants or desires. All I really knew was that he cared deeply for his home and wanted to stop its untimely destruction. Yet, he couldn't do that on his own.

I'd been driven to figure out who I was when I wasn't the alpha's daughter.

Together, even if it wasn't all sunshine and roses, I felt confident we were both going to get what we wanted.

Chapter Thirteen

CILLIAN

Having Dawsyn at my side eased a lot of my inner turmoil, but still, my mind couldn't stop thinking about everything she'd told me. Worse, I had no fucking clue what I was going to do about it.

The idea that my Nannio had turned on us in favor of a brother I'd never known existed burned. Why hadn't I been given a choice in the matter? To meet him and know why he was furious enough to kill thousands of people.

Knowing I wasn't going to get the answers I seeked anytime soon, I had to force those thoughts out of my mind. There was no changing the past. We had to figure out a way to stop whatever they were planning and keep future body counts to a minimum.

I took Dawsyn to meet with a few of the people I'd known Uncle Jerome trusted. The conversation was painful, but quick. I recapped everything. They asked Dawsyn questions about Earth and a few clarifying things about her time with Knox, then the conversation switched drastically.

Sereph, a childhood friend of my mother's, pointed toward the tunnels. "We don't have enough supplies to last us the next few days while we figure out our next steps." Her bright red hair made her fair skin stand out starkly in the dimly lit room.

"We should go now," Daron, Sereph's mate, said. "Before you came back and the attacks were at their worst, nights were the riskiest time to leave the cave."

"I can take Lykem and go," I said, hating the thought of leaving Dawsyn so soon, but at least she'd be safe here.

She laughed. "You think you're leaving me here while you go have all the fun?"

My brows pinched. "I wouldn't call what we need to do *fun*."

Dawsyn glanced at Sereph. "How did you get supplies before?"

My mate's confidence at speaking with the others amazed me. She wasn't afraid of this place or anything she'd experience. Besides her earlier breakdown, I'd seen nothing other than strength from the wolf shifter.

"We went out in groups of four or five," Sereph answered. "Two people would stay in their dragon forms, and we'd load them up with items to carry back."

"Perfect." Dawsyn grinned, looking over at me. "I can help load and you can be the pack mule."

"The what?" I asked.

She shook her head. "Clearly, animals between our two worlds don't cross over that much. When should we leave?"

Sereph and Daron shared a look, then glanced back at Mantha who had been rather quiet for most of the meeting.

She was one of the elders who had helped make

decisions alongside Uncle Jerome. She was well over a hundred years old, but her mind was still as sharp as ever.

Her back was to us, but she knew we were waiting on her opinion. Her grey hair fell to her clasped hands at the base of her spine, and her shoulders remained straight, but she didn't turn to us as she spoke.

"Go now, but only come back with what you can find within a half hour," she said, voice filled with concern. "We can't risk losing anyone else now that we know who we're dealing with."

The way she said "who" made me wonder if she knew more about this so-called brother of mine than she'd yet to say.

I'd been attempting to put the pieces of information together since Dawsyn told me what she knew. The only solution that made sense was that he had been my mother's child before I came along.

Her lineage was where my lightning energy came from. It seemed as if he'd acquired the same trait and was using my father's fire power to increase the destruction.

I had so many questions, ones Mantha might be able to answer, but it didn't seem as if she was in the mood to chat. She'd kept her back to us while inching closer to the exit of the room.

My other hope in getting answers was to rescue my father, assuming he was the same Darius that Dawsyn had mentioned, but taking care of the people here and making sure Dawsyn was safe had to take priority for the time being.

My eyes cast back to my mate. I wanted to tell her that she couldn't come with us, but if I was being honest, I knew she could handle herself. Having her close would actually make this easier.

"We'll take two groups," I said. "I'll still bring Lykem to help Dawsyn know what to help load, while Sereph and Daron grab what they can. Anything besides food and clothes needed?"

"That will be sufficient for now," Mantha said, then surprised at least me when she finally turned around, directing her silver eyes right to me. "What your grandmother chose to do has no reflection on you. I hope you know that."

I'd thought I did, but the relief that coursed through me once she said the words was something I hadn't known I needed.

I bowed my head briefly in respect. "Thank you."

She exited the room without another word, and it was just the four of us. Daron ran a hand over his jet-black hair. "We'll get the nets and meet you outside the caves?"

"That works. Lykem is near the portal, but I'll shift and call for him." I stood and grabbed Dawsyn's hand.

She followed without saying anything until we were in the tunnels again and going the opposite way as the others. "You're sure you can trust these people?"

"Why? Did something seem off to you?" I'd always thought I had good intuition, but seeing as my own grandmother had turned on us...

"No, but I don't understand the dynamic here, so I wanted to be sure," she said. "It's odd that there's no clear leader."

"We've never needed one, but then again, we've never faced something like this," I replied. "I can see how having one before now might have prevented some of this shit from happening."

She squeezed my hand. "Bad things happen all the time, even when there's a good leader."

We continued toward the cave exit that we'd come through previously, and I didn't stop until we came to a clearing big enough for me to shift.

Dawsyn stayed further back, her eyes on me and alight with curiosity. Her questions earlier about what I was capable of made me realize there was a lot we didn't know about each other, but that would change soon.

I quickly called my dragon forward and was careful not to stretch my wings or tail too far, knowing our mate was close.

We're going on a supply run, I said, searching out Lykem's energy. *I need you to help me with Dawsyn.*

You want me to babysit her? He chuckled. *Are you sure that's a good idea?*

My chest rumbled. *No. I want you to help her load the nets, you idiot. Are you and Penn almost done?*

Already on our way back. Be to you in less than five.

At least he knew when to joke and when not to. Most of the time.

I shifted back so that I could tell Dawsyn he'd be here soon, but she was laughing before I could say anything.

"You and your dragon get the same pinched expressions on your faces when you're annoyed," she said, then smiled widely. "It's adorable."

"How do you know I was annoyed?" I countered, closing the distance between us.

She took several steps forward, helping to do the same. "Because your chest rumbled at the same time."

"That could have been for many reasons." I kissed her softly, then made the same sound. "Like because I'm happy as well."

Her fingertip rubbed between my brows. "But when combined with this...you know I'm right. Don't be upset because I know you better than you know me."

I grabbed her by the hips and lifted her off the ground with ease until she was eye level with me. "You think so? Well, even if that's true, I'm stronger than you."

She barked out another laugh. "Stronger isn't always better. I proved that in the gym."

I was tempted to tell her that I'd let her win, but she was also right. I wanted her to keep that confidence. She'd escaped from Knox and had put up a good fight with me. Her inner wolf strength was more than enough to take care of them.

My dragon's spirit filled my chest, letting me know he more than agreed with that statement.

"Tell me more about you, then," I said. "What's your favorite thing to eat?"

She groaned, rubbing a hand over her stomach. "Everything. Food is life."

The sullen look on her face made me realize I hadn't given her the opportunity to clean up, change, or do anything since finding her in the forest. "Are you sure you want to go with us? I could have someone help you get settled here with new clothes and food."

Her fingers gripped my t-shirt, almost to the point I thought she might rip it. "Not a chance in hell, Mate."

Our foreheads were nearly touching as she pushed up on her toes, staring me down. I was one second from capturing her mouth and feasting on her when I sensed Lykem's dragon land.

"You're eating the second we get back," I said, still keeping her close.

"As long as you join me," she replied with a smirk.

Lykem gagged. "For all the dragon eggs, people. Am I going to have to deal with seeing you two all over each other every time we hang out?"

I didn't bother acknowledging him, but apparently, Dawsyn was fond of banter.

She glanced over at him, her grip still tight on my shirt. "If you think this is 'all over each other,' I wonder what you'd think of this."

Her lips crashed into mine and there was no way I wasn't going to kiss her back. Her tongue pushed forward, and I angled my head, pulling her closer.

"My eyes, they burn," he shouted, making Dawsyn laugh.

"He's entertaining."

"He's annoying at best," I replied.

Lykem huffed. "I can hear you."

I finally stepped back from Dawsyn. "We weren't trying to be quiet."

He threw a rope at Dawsyn's feet. "I brought that for you. Figured you might not hate riding your mate so much if you had a bit of security."

As confusion filled me, Dawsyn's face paled for the briefest of seconds, then she glared at him. "And here I thought I was going to like you."

He grinned. "You're going to love me. Obviously, not like Cillian, but a brotherly sort of love. It's impossible for people not to. I'm just that awesome."

"Alright, Lick-em," she jeered. "Whatever you say."

I grabbed her wrist, lightly tugging her toward me. "What did he mean about riding your mate?"

"First, that's actually a really inappropriate thing to say in the company of others." She narrowed her eyes, but the corners of her mouth lifted. "And I might have stretched the truth before when I told you it was fun flying over here on your back."

I raised a brow. "By how much?"

"By a lot," she admitted. "It was terrifying, but I'll get used to it. My wolf and I are just used to being on the ground."

My arms wrapped around her, and I held her close. "It's okay. If you want to use the rope, you can."

"Abso-fucking-lutely not." She held a finger up. "On second thought, I could use it to hang your friend from one of those trees by his ankles."

"I can still hear you," Lykem whined.

She glanced back at him and winked. "I know."

"You couldn't lift my body on your own, even if you got close enough to get the rope around me," Lykem taunted, and I knew the second the words left his mouth, he was going to regret them.

Dawsyn squared off with him. "Are you sure about that?"

He swallowed thickly. "Yep."

He wasn't at all, but before things could escalate,

Sereph and Daron joined us with the nets. "Everyone ready?" Sereph asked.

Lykem was the first to turn and move away from the trees to shift. "Been ready."

This was going to be interesting.

Chapter Fourteen

DAWSYN

Cillian wasn't willing to let my uneasiness with being uncomfortable on his back go. I'd been forced to use the rope and was sure that I'd be embarrassed in front of the other dragons. Yet, as I held the coarse material between my fingers, I was suddenly wondering what else we could do with this rope...

Though, it pained me to admit that Lykem had been right. I felt more comfortable on Cillian's back when I had something besides his scales to hold on to.

We flew through the sky, but instead of taking in the sights, I took this time to catch up with my wolf given how quiet she'd been.

How are you doing? I asked.

Better, but I can still feel Knox.

Yeah, so could I and I didn't like it, but there wasn't anything we could do about that until we saw my parents.

Rejecting mates wasn't something that happened often. Very few people even knew how it was done. I'd thought I could do it with pure will, but after having a bond actually completed and feeling Knox so deeply rooted in my soul, I knew it wasn't going to be that simple.

Mom or even GiGi will help, I said.

Then, we can bond with our dragon.

Yes, and not that I've changed my mind, but is there reason to rush things? Not that I didn't want to bond with Cillian, but I wanted the decision to be on our terms and not because we were forced to.

I could hear the eyeroll in her tone. *It would prevent any other dragons from making you their mate.*

Okay, she had a point.

We'll figure that out later. One thing at a time. Let's get these dragons their supplies.

Cillian's dragon came down for a landing, once again smooth and easy. I released the rope that stayed tied around his neck, then jumped down. By the time my feet were on the ground, Lykem was already waiting for me.

"Ready, Wolf Girl?" he quipped, spreading out the net we'd brought and securing it to Cillian's back leg.

I turned to Cillian and his neck bent toward me until our heads were just inches apart. "I'll be right back."

There was something in his eyes like fear, but it was also mixed with understanding. He knew I was capable, and I was thankful he hadn't tried to force me to stay behind.

My palm rubbed between his eyes, careful to avoid the sharp horns at the top. "We'll be quick. I promise," I said to my mate first, then I turned back to Lykem. "Ready, Dragon *Boy*."

He smirked, then headed toward an unmarked building.

I regretfully left Cillian's dragon and followed Lykem. "Where are we?"

The structures around us were spread out and very few of them damaged. There weren't any homes, just commercial buildings, yet none of them were marked.

"Textile processing center." He jerked the door open. "We're going to get clothing and bedding first, then we'll head next door and see what's left in the utility building."

Clothes would be nice. I'd have to keep an eye out for something I could borrow. Even I was getting a little tired of smelling the stench of the clothes I'd been donning for a week.

Though, I was going to need a shower—or more likely, a trip to a river or lake to wash up—before I put new clothes on.

I followed Lykem into the nearest building. It was dark, but my wolf eyes quickly adjusted. There were large machines that I'd never seen before and had no idea what exactly they did, but beyond those were large wooden crates filled to the brim with sheets and blankets. That was where we headed.

We moved with urgency and Lykem started tossing me items. "Let me know when you've had enough."

This time there was no snark in his words. We were all business now. Get in, get what was needed, and get the hell out.

Once the pile was about a foot over my head, I finally tapped out. "I'll go throw this in the net and come back to help you."

He didn't respond. Just started gathering as many items as he could into his own arms.

I moved my legs as fast as I could without worrying about the pile that I was carrying tumbling to the ground. Thankfully, the door was easily kicked open and I headed straight for Cillian.

Peeking around the mound, I found him staring up into the sky, likely watching for anyone—or anything—who wasn't supposed to be up there.

I dropped the items onto the net as planned, briefly ran my hand over the scales on his side, then raced back inside.

Lykem was just coming out of the door, his load nearly as big as mine had been. "One more each," he said.

I nodded and headed inside to get started like I'd seen him doing. Except, just as I reached the box, the ground beneath my feet vibrated.

I braced myself for a moment, then listened. The first noise to reach me was that of a dragon's roar.

Cillian.

Without thinking about anything else, I ran back toward the exit and shoved the door open just in time to see a fireball dropping from the sky, headed right toward where I stood in the doorway.

There was nowhere for me to hide. I wasn't going to outrun the massive magical meteor-looking fireball.

There was a fleeting thought to race to the back of the building, but before I could fully turn around, Cillian's dragon made an animalistic noise, then...motherfucking lightning shot from his mouth.

The energy was white and mystical and came out in a stream that wrapped around the fireball, squeezing tightly around the ball of destruction until it imploded in the sky before I could be burned to death.

Holy shit. That was...incredible.

I ran out of the building. Lykem was nowhere to be seen, but I was headed for my mate anyway. His chest was heaving, and as soon as I was close enough to him, his wing curved around me, tucking my body against his.

Embers dropped from the sky around us, and I realized he was protecting me from getting burned.

I pressed my forehead against his cool, smooth scales and wrapped my arms around him as best I could, soaking in the bond I couldn't actually feel any longer, but that I could still recall from before.

Lykem popped up from under Cillian's body. "Time to go. More of these things are coming."

I didn't need to hear anything else. I swung myself onto Cillian's back, grabbed the rope, and patted his spine, indicating I was ready.

Within seconds, we were airborne. When I looked back, I wanted to rage on behalf of all the dragons here.

More buildings were burning. Five in total. One being just two over from where I'd been.

Lykem flew next to us, and we stayed low, moving at much faster speeds than before. When I checked for Sereph and Daron, I didn't see them, but there were three more fireballs that shot out of the dark forest and were aimed right where we'd been.

One thing I did know was that Knox was a coward. Through and through.

He'd had to blackmail me with the life of my best friend to get to me. He'd used someone else's magic to harm others, and he seemed to rarely leave that underground bunker.

He was fucked now, because I knew where he was. It didn't matter that I wasn't sure how we were going to get in. All I knew was that we would. And when we did, Knox would cease to exist.

When we got back, Sereph and Daron were already there, shifted back to their human forms and untangling their net, which wasn't filled with as much stuff as I knew we'd been hoping for.

Cillian kneeled down just before I jumped. I moved to untie the ropes from him, but his body began to shimmer. As soon as I could blink, he was back on two feet and wrapping his arms tightly around me.

I hugged him back, not needing the bond to know that he needed this contact. "I'm so sorry," he muttered into my hair.

"What are you sorry for?" I tried to push him back to look at his face, but he wouldn't relent on his hold.

"That fireball never should have gotten so close to you," he said. "I panicked and didn't react as quickly as I should have."

I finally used enough force to shove him back. "You stopped it and that's all that matters. Don't ever apologize for saving me again." My voice was stern, my eyes narrow, and I poked my finger into his chest several times. "Do you understand?"

His hands gripped my face, almost painfully. "Do you understand that I can't lose you?"

The pain in his voice nearly broke me. I did understand. I was just really good at putting my emotions into a box and not letting them out. Most of the time.

Cillian wore his heart on his sleeve, which only made

me want him more. It made me believe that I could trust him with not only my life, but my own heart.

I pushed up onto my toes and kissed him hard, my fingers threading through his hair that had grown out at least half an inch since I'd met him.

Our tongues tangled, and he pushed closer to me, pressing his palm against the base of my spine. He tasted sweet, but there was so much longing in his movements, all I could focus on was giving back to him.

If we had the bond, he'd understand my feelings better. He'd know it didn't matter how many times he paused or panicked. I knew he would be there for me if he was capable.

And if he wasn't… Well, there was nothing we could do about that. Sometimes fate was too strong.

Our kisses eased out of the desperation stage, and I finally pulled back, but only far enough to speak. "We should help them take everything inside."

"It's already done."

I glanced around to find both nets empty except for one pile of clothes. Keeping a hold on Cillian's hand, I guided us forward, then bent down.

A plain black tee and blue jeans, both a size too big, but appreciated nonetheless, were sitting there. Underneath them were what I assumed to be new underwear and socks. I grabbed the cotton material, never more thankful for clothes than I was in that moment.

Living in my own filth for nearly a week was hard to ignore. Though, it was a little awkward thinking that Lykem likely left them for me.

"Is there somewhere I can wash up around here?" I asked, looking back up at Cillian.

He nodded toward the trees. "About a mile past the cave entrance."

"Are you up for a walk, because I'd really love to be clean."

His fingers brushed against my cheek. "Whatever you want."

Mother shittery shit. He was killing me with his kindness. Only this wasn't a death I wanted to avoid.

We walked toward the trees, hand-in-hand as he led the way. Being with him in the quiet of nature felt oddly calming, considering we'd just run from a warzone.

"Do you usually go back after the attacks? Try to put out the fires?" I asked, wondering if there was any hope of minimizing the damages.

He shrugged. "I don't know. There weren't any while you were with Knox. That was the first one I've been around for."

"We should do that when we're back if nobody has." All I could picture were people's homes burning and them coming home to nothing other than despair. After living in the caves for however long, nobody deserved that.

Well, except for Knox. He deserved dead fly sprinkles on his shit sundae.

Within ten minutes, we were at a small pond. The water was so clear that I could see the pebbled bottom. I took off my shoes but stopped as Cillian started speaking.

"You might want to test the waters and see how badly you want to be clean," he said with a grimace. "I didn't think to tell you that the nearest water comes from the snow melt on the mountain above the caves."

Not at all what I wanted to hear, but there was no way I was going to dip a toe in beforehand. I needed to be clean. I'd just have to jump in and hope for the best.

Though, I did have another idea.

"Why don't you join me so we can keep each other warm?" I asked. "You know. Shared body heat and all that."

I wasn't sure it was a good idea to be naked with Cillian given I still had a bond with that monster of a dragon, but I couldn't pass up the opportunity. Not when it so nicely presented itself.

With one tug, he had his shirt pulled over his head and hands on the button of his pants. "Don't mind if I do."

The smirk on his face as he held my gaze had my eagerness tripling.

I stripped my clothes off in record time, unconcerned with my nakedness. Sure, our shifter magic allowed us to keep our clothes intact when we transformed, but that didn't mean we were shy about our bodies.

Though, when my eyes landed on Cillian's, I realized I'd yet to even see his chest before now. My eyes unashamedly roamed over his wide shoulders, down to his pecs, then to his abs. They rippled under my scrutiny, making me think that even his abs had abs thanks to all the dips and curves.

Finally, saving the best for last, I took in the goods. His cock was more than half-mast, and my fingers itched to wrap the increasing length.

He cleared his throat. "Eyes up here, Dawsyn. I'm not fucking you in frigid water."

"That doesn't mean we can't play." I smirked and ran

toward him, naked body be damned. I leapt into his arms, wrapping my legs around his waist and holding on to his neck. "Let's go in together."

He groaned. "You're going to kill me before we're even bonded."

"Possibly, but at least you'll die happy."

Chapter Fifteen

CILLIAN

For the briefest of moments, I'd thought I was going to lose Dawsyn. That there was nothing I could do to save her. That her death would be my fault.

Those thoughts had paralyzed me until I remembered that was a lie.

Using my lightning energy should have been second nature to me. I didn't know what had caused me to panic, but it couldn't, and wouldn't, happen again.

Holding her in my arms was the only thing that had calmed my racing heart. Though, having her naked and clinging to my body kicked things right back up.

The desire to take her right there on the cold ground was so fucking strong. I wanted to sink right into her warmth and never come back from the euphoria I knew I'd find there. Yet, I couldn't forget that she was still bonded to Knox. Even if he'd never touched her, it felt...not right.

I wanted Dawsyn to be all mine when I claimed her. Not just her heart, but her body and most importantly, her soul.

I carried her to the water, my balls feeling like they'd been shoved up to my throat as soon as they were submerged in the iciness. Though, not even the nearly freezing temperatures could stop my dick from trying to reach Dawsyn's ass.

Her smile took my breath away as I inched her into the water. At least until she was finally wet. Her nails dug into my shoulders. "Mother shittery shit! Just dunk me!"

There was a fleeting thought that I'd pay for this later, but I did as she asked, and she flailed in my arms.

As her legs still clung to me, I used my hands to rub over her skin, cleaning her as well and quick as was possible. She scrubbed her hair, tilting her head back and giving me a full-frontal view of her chest.

I couldn't help myself. I had to make sure every inch of her was clean. I palmed her breasts and squeezed, pinching her hardened nipples between my fingers.

Her ankles tightened around my waist, and she groaned. "I think I just forgot how fucking frigid it is in here."

I dipped my head forward, doing exactly what I said I didn't want to do. My mouth covered one of her pert nipples and sucked hard before letting my teeth lightly scrape over the sensitive skin.

"Fuck me," she muttered.

I grinned, because I had a feeling that she was speaking both literally and figuratively.

Even though I wasn't keen on having sex with her for the first time while she was still tied to someone else, that didn't mean I couldn't fuck her in other ways.

I walked us back toward the shore until only my legs

were still immersed in the pond. She shivered in my arms, leaning her head back against my shoulder. "I need all your body heat now."

"Everything that's mine is yours." My lips pressed over her forehead, and I slipped a hand between us.

Her hold around my waist loosened and she lifted her head. "Whatcha doing down there?"

"Sharing my body heat," I replied, my fingers brushing over her folds that were already plenty warm.

"Hmmm." She licked her lips. "I don't oppose."

"I didn't think you would." I pressed further down, pushing one finger inside her. She instantly contracted around me.

"Fuck," she hissed, shifting her hips to give me more room.

My left arm was wrapped around her ass, my palm splayed out to help keep her up while I let my other hand have all the fun.

My finger moved in and out, slow and steady. She was tight, but wet and ready.

She held on around my neck, beginning to rock against my hand in time with my movements. "More," she groaned.

I wasn't sure if she meant another finger or faster motions, but I gave her both regardless.

Using the hold she had around my waist, Dawsyn leveraged her body and then came back down on my hand. "Fucking hell. I don't think anything has ever felt so good."

Her body was covered in gooseflesh, but she didn't seem the least bit bothered by the cold any longer.

"This is only the beginning," I promised, whispering into her ear just before I skimmed my teeth over her lobe.

My fingers continued to pump in and out of her, and she rode my hand like it was a grand champion horse.

The inner walls of her pussy began to twitch, and her head fell back once again. Using my thumb, I applied the slightest amount of pressure to her clit, and her eyes shot open while the rest of her body tensed within my hold.

Her mouth formed into an O, and she cried out, grinding harder against me.

I kept up the dual motions, fucking her with my hand and reminding myself of my earlier words. This was only the beginning of us. I had the rest of our lives to devour this beautiful woman. This right here would be enough. For now.

She came apart in my arms, her body becoming dead weight against me and forcing me to hold her with both hands.

I guided her upper body back up and pressed her head against my shoulder as I walked us out of the water. My legs were nearly numb, but the rest of me was on fire.

Bending down, I reached for my shirt and used it to begin drying her off. At least, I did until she took it from me.

"What are you doing?" she asked, tone accusing.

"Uh. Helping you get dressed before you freeze to death."

At the mention of the cooler weather, she shivered in my arms. "We're not done here."

I grinned and kissed her quickly. "Yes, we are."

She reached underneath her legs, her fingers wrapping around my cock. "He says otherwise."

"*He* is more patient than you seem to think." At least, I

hoped so. Two hard-ons with no relief in a matter of hours wasn't ideal.

"What if I'm not?" Her mouth downturned, and she squeezed harder around me.

I pushed her shirt over her head. "You're going to have to figure that out on your own. I'm not fucking you out here."

She snorted and pulled the clothing from her face. "You sort of just did."

"And if I let you touch me anymore, I'm going to really *did*." I gripped her chin. "I'd prefer you to be *all* mine when I claim you. Do you understand?"

She leaned into my touch and released my cock from her grip. "I do. I don't like it, but I do."

My hand smacked over her still-wet ass. "Good. Now, let's get you into some fresh clothes."

She wiggled out of my hold and stood on a rock next to us, using my shirt to dry off the rest of her body as well as she could. I handed her underwear and jeans over, and she shivered. "These clothes aren't near as warm as you are."

I smiled and nodded, fighting through the desire to strip her naked again. "They will be in a few minutes."

While she finished dressing, I did the same minus my shirt that she was now using to wring the water from her long hair.

"I hope you didn't need this." She dangled the black material between us once she was done.

"I have more back in the caves."

She raised a brow. "More black shirts? I'm pretty sure that's all I've ever seen you wear."

"Makes getting dressed every day easy. Though, I think I have a grey one somewhere."

She brushed past me. "You're such a guy."

My hand found her ass again. "And now you match me."

Her eyes cast down, and she groaned. "I do. Please tell me that not all dragons wear black."

I wanted to lie and say yes just to mess with her, but I couldn't keep a straight face. "No. We'll get you something different once we're back."

She frowned. "I don't want to take anything from the others. Maybe I can have Beatrix help us bring other stuff back that we need here and couldn't get earlier."

That was something I should have thought of. I was touched that Dawsyn had.

She might have run from her pack, but she cared about people much more than she let on.

"That would be really appreciated, as long as your family doesn't want to kill me any longer," I said as we started walking back toward the cave.

Her fingers wrapped around my arm, and she leaned her head against my shoulder. "They're smart enough not to piss me off *that* much."

I wasn't sure what that meant, but I had a feeling one day I would find out.

We got back to the tunnels, and I headed for the space I'd claimed as mine first so I could get a shirt. My blood might have run hot, but that didn't mean I didn't want to be clothed most of the time.

"Clearly, you're not fucking anything here," Dawsyn

muttered, likely not approving of the sheets for walls and blankets subbing as a mattress.

"No, definitely not here," I said with a chuckle.

Her eyes met mine and she shrugged. "Didn't mean to say that out loud, but at least we're on the same page."

With a shake of my head, I reached into my bag, grabbed a new—also black—shirt, and slipped it over my head. "Let's go find Lykem. We'll see if they intend to send anyone out to check on the fires."

Dawsyn rubbed her hands over her face. "I completely forgot about that."

"We needed a moment out there." I wrapped an arm around her shoulders and pressed my lips to the top of her head.

She looked back up at me, eyes bright. "We really did. At least I did. I don't stink anymore, and I got dessert."

Lykem came around the corner, nearly running into us. "Did you bring me dessert?"

Dawsyn laughed and nudged my side with her elbow. "I don't know. Did you save any *dessert* for your friend?"

"No." I deadpanned, not enjoying her sense of humor in the slightest.

"Sorry, Dragon Boy," Dawsyn joked. "Maybe next time."

"Maybe never," I muttered.

Lykem seemed more confused than ever, but thankfully let the conversation end there. "We're going to go back out there. Do the two of you want to come?"

Dawsyn answered first. "Yes. Are we checking on the structures?"

He nodded. "And getting some flour for Greta. She's out and says we won't have food tomorrow without it."

"Best not to piss off the cook," I agreed.

"Oh, and Ceera gave me this for you." Lykem handed Dawsyn a bag.

When she opened it, I got a glimpse of a toothbrush and a comb. The latter was in her hand before she even finished saying thank you. "My hair was going to be a rat's nest tomorrow if I didn't brush it."

Lykem glanced at me. "Wolves are weird."

"She could still kick your ass," I said as Dawsyn quickly untangled her hair.

He barked out a laugh. "We'll have to test that theory soon."

My chest rumbled. No, we wouldn't. I didn't think my dragon would survive seeing another man put hands on our mate anytime soon. Even if it was all in good fun.

Chapter Sixteen

DAWSYN

Outside of the annoyance caused by the tie I still had to Knox, I was finally feeling like myself again. The dragons were kind, and helping them brought me a sense of peace I hadn't felt in years.

Peace like I used to have in the pack before my "help" began to feel forced...expected. Through reflection in the few weeks I'd been away from home, though, I understood that most of it had been on me and not the pack. Or even my parents.

I had allowed myself to be labeled "the alpha's daughter." I could have changed things without leaving, but I didn't regret my choice. Even with all the hell that had happened, I had found my mate and understood more about who I wanted to be, all within the short time I'd been gone.

After we'd saved one building, we found the others that had been hit were a lost cause. The group of six that had come this time decided to split up, and I gladly stayed with

Cillian, especially after he suggested we stop by his house to check for any useful supplies.

It was only a few blocks from where we'd been, and when he'd pointed to the small structure, I couldn't stop myself from smiling.

Cillian felt bigger than the whole world to me at times. He commanded so much attention and space. Yet, his home was more of a cottage and not at all what I expected.

The tan exterior was framed by dark wood, and there were two windows centered outside the wooden door. Grass grew tall within the yard, threatening to take over the stone pathway, but there were no flowers or bushes. That part at least made sense to me.

He opened the front door and stepped back for me to go in first. "After you."

I entered his home to find minimal furniture and open spaces. There was a living room on my left. A fireplace surrounded by dark stone filled the middle of the main wall, and only one couch sat in front of it. A coffee table was positioned between them with a deck of cards on top.

"You play games?" I asked, intrigued by this fact.

He shrugged and glanced to my right. "Before all this, it could be boring here at times."

He was embarrassed. That was adorable.

My eyes went toward a small kitchen, one not much bigger than what was in the dorms. "Not much of a cooker, huh?"

"Noodles don't require much to make, and I barbeque my meat out back," he answered.

Carbs and protein diet. Wasn't surprised about that either.

Moving on from there, I walked through the living room to the only door I could see. It led straight into what I assumed to be the master bedroom.

A king-sized bed was front and center when I entered, covered with a chocolate-colored comforter and cream pillows. At least he knew how to match things.

To the right of that was a sliding door that led to the patio. I could see the barbeque he mentioned sitting out there and wondered how often he merely relaxed under the stars.

On the opposite side of the room were two more doors, which I assumed led to his bathroom and closet, but I'd done enough invading of his space and didn't bother to inspect those areas. Instead, I jumped onto his bed, letting my body sink into the mattress.

It was like a cloud. Every muscle inside me relaxed, and I briefly closed my eyes. "I'm not leaving this spot."

Cillian stepped forward, pushed my knees apart that were draped over the edge of the mattress, and stood between my legs. He leaned forward, placing a hand on both sides of my ribs. "I wish we could stay, but I'm just going to grab a few things we could use in the caves, then we need to get back."

I leaned up on my elbows. "Because we have no idea where the next fireball is going to strike?"

He nodded. "Given what we know now, I'm surprised my house is still standing."

There was an odd emotion in my chest, but I ignored it. "Maybe we could just stay a little while longer..."

I'd have loved to continue what we started in the water, which wasn't going to happen back in the cave.

I sat up further, bringing my hands in front of me and placing them on Cillian's chest. His muscles rippled under my touch, so I continued, lowering my hands until they could travel beneath his shirt.

"What are you doing, Dawsyn?" His words held that delicious growl I enjoyed so much.

"Exploring."

As soon as the word left my mouth, there was a sharper pain in my chest. I sucked in a breath and squeezed my eyes closed as I tried to figure out what was happening.

It's Knox, my wolf said. *He's trying to get to you through the bond.*

Fuck.

"What's wrong?" Cillian asked, gripping my shoulders as I folded in on myself.

I held up a finger so I could sort it out with my wolf first.

I thought that was a fated mate thing. Chosen mates aren't supposed to have all the added benefits.

A downfall of not being patient enough or trusting fate to put you on the path to the one meant for you.

You're right, but that doesn't mean he isn't trying. I can sense him everywhere. Almost as if he's getting closer.

He can track us. I'd known that about mates. I should have remembered that. *Damn it!*

We need to go, she said, but I was already pushing Cillian back, telling him the same thing.

"Why? What's happening?" he asked, not moving as quickly as I would have liked.

"Knox. You were right to want to wait for anything with me until I was no longer tied to him." Saying those words gutted me. I wanted my fated mate and only him. The fact that I couldn't have him because of that psychotic dragon had murderous thoughts running rampant through my mind.

He grabbed my shoulders and forced me to slow down. "Hey. What he did changes nothing. You are still mine and I'm yours."

"Yeah. Well, your brother isn't too pleased about that," I said. "I think he's trying to find me."

Cillian's lip curled up in disgust. "He's not my brother."

Poor choice of words on my part, but that was the least of our worries. "We need to go before he finds your house and destroys that, too."

I grabbed his hand and pulled him to the front of the house, but he stopped just before the door. "What if we waited for him?"

My head turned back. "Fight him now? Just the two of us?"

He nodded, and I couldn't deny that the idea had merit. Yet, there was something bothering me.

Knox had no control over you before, my wolf said. *But he's using some sort of magic to strengthen your bond. We have no way to know the ramifications of that.*

That fucking bastard.

"I don't think it's a good idea to be around Knox until I've severed ties with him," I said, not wanting to stress Cillian with my wolf's revelations. "Let's put that plan into action once we're back from seeing my family."

He didn't seem pleased but didn't argue. Mostly. "I want him dead for what he did."

"I know, and he will be. In time." At least, I fucking hoped so.

Cillian grabbed my hand, and we exited his home together. I'd wanted to ask if I could run back as my wolf, but given the tugging in my chest that I knew was coming from Knox, I didn't bother. Sticking as close to Cillian as possible seemed like the best choice.

He shifted right there in front of his house, and I wasted no time climbing onto his back. As he took flight, I held on to his scales as well as I could since we'd forgotten the rope when we left.

His right wing dropped down, forcing his body to dodge in the same direction. I nearly pissed my pants and screamed at him not to play around, but as soon as we leveled out again, I realized what had him making those moves.

Lightning was shooting across the sky. Streams of darker silver sparks that looked similar to what I'd seen come from Cillian earlier that day, and yet, they didn't at all make me feel safe.

Knox is attacking again, my wolf said.

How the hell do you know and I don't?

Because I can feel his dragon, too.

Wasn't she just full of revelations, suddenly.

I didn't bother to relay the information to Cillian. He seemed very aware of what was happening. All I could do was focus on not falling off his back. I kept my feet planted where his wings met his body and leaned forward so that my chest was laying against the base of his neck and I could reach the longer, more spike-like humps.

Once I had a solid hold and wasn't worried about

falling off, I yelled into the air. "I'm not falling off anytime soon. Do whatever you need to."

As soon as the words left my mouth, my stomach ended up in my throat. Cillian's dragon tilted his body downward, and I had what felt like a literal killer view of the ground. He swooped left just before we crashed into the surface, then right, and I glanced behind us.

I couldn't see anyone else, and there were only faint flickers of the lightning left behind.

When I thought we were out of the woods, a shadow fell over us, and I yelled once again. "Above us!"

Cillian was already fully aware. We went vertical again, this time going higher into the sky.

The dull sun was cresting over the mountains in the distance, but still provided enough light for us to see Knox's deep emerald dragon behind us.

At least, I assumed it was Knox based on the sensations in my chest increasing.

His dragon's teeth snapped, trying to grab hold of Cillian's tail, but my true mate was faster and kept just enough distance between them.

I focused on keeping my hold to Cillian secure. The last thing we needed was for me to fall off and Knox to be the one to catch me.

I assumed Cillian was going to attempt to outrun Knox, but not even a minute later, his body curved, turning us around and coming face to face with his brother.

He had to be fucking insane, but I didn't say a word. Instead, I paid as much attention as I could to the warring dragons.

Cillian's left wing swung out, and the sharp point cut into Knox's face, drawing blood.

Knox roared and flicked his tail around, just missing me.

This had Cillian fuming. Or I assumed so based on the smoking huffs coming out of his nose.

I was waiting for him to use his lightning ability, but that moment never came.

Knox came for us again, and Cillian dropped his wings, sending us plummeting to the ground. Knox was right behind us. His claws skimmed the ends of my hair that were currently above my head. "Move!" I yelled at Cillian, unsure if he was aware just how close our opponent was.

Except we were too close to the trees and there wasn't anywhere to go other than up, right into Knox's path.

Cillian continued with his current trajectory, right into the ground. I had no clue what he was thinking, but if he got me scalped by the fucking claws still reaching for my head, he was going to suffer. Immensely.

Right after I killed Knox.

Trees were right in front of us. Knox was still above us and the ground was below. We could turn around, but the time that would take would allow Knox to have the upper hand.

I wanted to scream at Cillian, but I held tight, hoping he was about to unveil some superpower I wasn't aware he had.

Just as I was certain we were going to crash right into the trees, Lykem's dragon came out of nowhere and plowed into Knox. As soon as that happened, Cillian's wings went out, slowing his speed. He turned around, taking me further and further away.

I glanced back to see Lykem blocking Knox from attacking and their two dragons going head to head.

Fuck. Lykem better be fine. I wasn't going to be okay if we'd run and gotten Cillian's best friend killed.

Chapter Seventeen

CILLIAN

I should have known better. I shouldn't have kept Dawsyn at my house for longer than a minute. Hell, we shouldn't have even bothered going. There wasn't anything there that I needed, but telling her no when she'd wanted so badly to see where I lived was hard.

Knox had almost gotten to her. Again. I'd nearly failed to protect her. Again.

The rage filling me wasn't going to lessen anytime soon.

If I hadn't had Dawsyn with me, I'd have killed the fucker right then and there, but there was no way I was going to risk my mate getting caught in the crossfire, which was also why I didn't use my lightning against Knox. I was too afraid of her getting burned from the energy while she was on my back.

As we raced back to the caves, I knew we had to do something about their connection, and soon. I hadn't even had her back for a full day, and he'd already come for her.

The bond she had with him needed to be fucking severed.

As soon as we were close enough to the caves, I landed and Dawsyn jumped off of me. Her entire body was shaking, and her eyes were wide.

I shifted back to my human form and went straight to her, holding her painfully tight against my chest. "I'm so fucking sorry."

"That had nothing to do with you," she growled. Her anger that I had mistaken for fear was suddenly palpable.

"I need to get you out of here," I said, pressing my lips to the top of her head and anchoring her to me. "He can't get that close to you again."

"We're meeting my family tomorrow," she said. "We'll figure something out then."

I shook my head. "No. Tonight. I won't risk him coming after you again while everyone is sleeping."

She leaned back, heavy emotions washing over her eyes as she stared up at me. "I'm going to get everyone killed."

"No. This is all on him." If anything, I'd started this war simply by being born. Whatever vendetta Knox had, it started with my family. Dawsyn was merely leverage he was trying to use, but I wasn't going to let him.

"You're sure we can go tonight?" she asked, glancing behind me and up into the sky. "As soon as we find out if Lykem is okay."

My hands still shook, so I kept them pressed against her back as I nodded. "I'm sure he's on his way back already."

I wanted to go help Lykem, but the thought of leaving Dawsyn made my stomach churn and scales threaten to burst from my skin.

Her stare met mine again, and she lightly rubbed her palms over my biceps. "We're okay." With those two words, all the ire I'd seen flitting within her eyes washed away. I tried to match her mood, but it wasn't happening.

She moved her touch to my chest. "I'm yours, Cillian. All yours. No matter what Knox did or does in the future. Nothing will change the fact that you're my mate. The only one I want."

"What if I can't protect you from him?" I asked, because that terror was what prevented me from calming down. It didn't matter how much we wanted each other, or how I'd burn the whole world for her. If I wasn't enough to keep her safe, none of that would make a difference.

Her hands cupped my neck and my chest rumbled. "Do not let fear take over. We will fight. For however long we have to. And we will win."

She wrapped her arms tighter around me and pulled herself up and into my arms. The phantom thrum of our bond twitched inside my chest—not actually there but knowing it should be.

I leaned forward and captured her mouth. She parted for me, and I wasted no time tasting her. One hand palmed her ass, keeping her up, and the other moved slowly up her sides until my thumb brushed underneath her breast.

The sensation elicited a gasp from her, which I devoured with our kiss.

She gripped my hair, angling my head and deepening the kiss.

Fuck, I needed to have this woman more than I needed my next breath. These kisses and touches weren't enough. I had to claim her. I had to know she was mine. All fucking mine and that nobody could ever take her from me again.

The sound of branches snapping had both of us jerking

apart. I kept Dawsyn in my hold as I turned around, just in time to see Lykem's dragon crash into the ground.

I set her down, grabbed her shoulders, and spoke firmly. "Go to the cave. Call for anyone who is nearest to you and tell them we need a healer right the fuck now."

She didn't hesitate. Didn't ask questions. Just turned and ran in the opposite direction.

My chest strained with tension as I hurried toward Lykem. He hadn't shifted back, which wasn't fucking good.

Blood coated his face, but I couldn't tell if it was his or someone else's. His right wing was ripped, and there were several deep gouges on his sides. Worse, there was still more crimson leaking out from underneath him.

Hell, I didn't even know how he'd made it back to us.

My hands pressed against his head, wiping what I could away from his eyes. "You're going to be okay. Dawsyn went to get a healer."

He made an odd noise that didn't make me feel any better, then fell to his side. I pulled my shirt off and went to his side, hoping to staunch the worst of the wounds with the fabric. But I froze when I moved around his wing.

I was going to fucking kill Knox ten times over for the damage he'd caused, but for this, seeing my oldest friend split open like a goddamned fish, he'd fucking burn.

Lykem's underbelly had a two-foot gaping wound, so deep that I could see severed muscles and what I assumed to be his guts.

The only thing keeping me from losing my damned mind was that none of his internal organs looked damaged.

His dragon healing would help, but without a healer, this amount of damage would kill Lykem within the hour.

As it was, I had a feeling he was going to need a blood donation.

Knowing there was nothing I could do for his stomach, I went to the wing that looked broken. This was going to hurt like a son of a bitch, but the bones had to be reset sooner rather than later, or he was never going to fly right again.

I glanced over at his dragon's face to find his eyes closed. Hopefully, he was passed out and would stay that way for this part.

My hands grabbed on to the end of his wing and steadied my grip. I took a deep breath as I made sure there was only the one break. I didn't want to fix one part only to make another worse. When I didn't see any other sections bent in the wrong direction, I twisted then pulled, fast and hard.

Bones rebroke from having already begun to heal, and Lykem's dragon reawakened with a boisterous roar.

His front legs swiped out, likely looking for anyone he could skewer for what I'd just done to him. At least one of his claws caught on my jeans, ripping the material, but just missing my skin.

I backed up and held my hands out. "It's just me, Lykem. I had to reset your wing."

Smoke puffed from his nostrils in a clear "fuck you," but I didn't take it personally. I'd have done the same thing.

His chest heaved, and I walked around him once again, seeing if there was anything else I could do. Before I could put hands on him again, Winter, our clan healer, came running back out with Dawsyn right behind her.

They had matching gasps when they saw Lykem.

Though, it was Dawsyn who dropped to her knees. "I'm so fucking sorry."

I went to her and pulled her back. "Not your fault." Then, I glanced at Winter. "What do you need?"

"Everything," she whispered, her hands hovering over his chest. "He's very weak, and his stomach..." She glanced back at me, a piece of her white-blonde hair falling over her wide aqua eyes. "This isn't good."

Dawsyn's body shook within my hold. "What can we do?"

"Tell Greta I need three full kits," Winter said. "She'll know what to do."

Dawsyn took off without me, and I stayed behind in case Winter needed my help to move Lykem.

As she bent next to him, the healer did a partial shift and began painfully plucking scales from her arm, creating a pile of at least a dozen. It wasn't well known outside of our clan that her scales held a healing power, but I was damned grateful I knew.

She placed three of them inside Lykem's stomach wound, then turned to me. "I need you to come and press his skin back together as close as you can get it. We need the magic from the scales to penetrate as deeply as possible."

There was no hesitation in following her request. My hands were already covered in blood, and if Lykem didn't recover from this...I knew I'd never unseen the gore we were surrounded by.

His dragon twitched, but it appeared he was passed out again. A small thanks.

Dawsyn returned, chest likely heaving from all the running and adrenaline. "Greta said she'd send the first kit out within five minutes and keep working on the others, but she's not sure if we have enough items to do three."

Winter cursed under her breath. "If you believe in a god, I'd start praying."

My mate's face paled. "What can I do?"

"Come over here and help me adjust his wing, so I can get to another wound."

I opened my mouth to tell Winter I would help. Lykem was a big dragon—heavy as shit—but before the words could get out, Dawsyn was at Lykem's shoulders and bent at the knees, sliding her hands beneath him.

With a loud grunt of effort, she lifted his upper body. Her face was red, and I was pretty sure she wasn't breathing, but hell, she was fucking strong.

Winter had him adjusted within thirty seconds, and Dawsyn dropped his body, wincing when the ground shook. "Sorry. Again," she whispered to him, rubbing her hand over his neck.

"He didn't feel a thing," Winter said, then handed her a few scales. "Place one of these in each of the wounds on his other side. If they don't look like they're going to close on their own, hold them together until you see the skin start to stitch itself back together."

"What happens when we get all the wounds closed?" Dawsyn asked.

"We pray he wakes up."

Chapter Eighteen

DAWSYN

It had been four hours since Lykem had come back. Once all of his injuries were sealed—thanks to Winter's scales—she'd covered his body with a balm made from the healing kits Greta had sent out. All that was left to do was to watch over him.

Dragons were sent to keep an eye out for any incoming attacks. We had no clue what happened to Knox since Lykem hadn't woken back up, but if he wasn't worse than Lykem, then we had to be prepared for anything.

Especially since the bastard seemed to have a beacon on me, thanks to our bond.

I badly wanted to leave and go home to find a way to break the connection, but more than that, I needed to know I hadn't killed Lykem.

Sure, I knew it wasn't me who'd wounded him, but Knox had only attacked because I was out there.

Cillian's thumb rubbed over the back of my hand. "We'll need to leave in the morning, even if he's not awake."

I tilted my head at him. "Can you read minds? I was just thinking about that."

His responding smile didn't quite reach his eyes. "No, but I've been thinking about it, too. The sooner we can cut the connection Knox forced on you, the better for everyone."

There was one thought that had come to my mind, and while neither my wolf nor I liked the idea, I felt the need to express it.

"What if I didn't cut the tie and used it against him like he is us?" I asked. The words made me want to vomit, but we had to be smart about this situation. Knox currently had the advantage, and we had to find some way to take that from him.

Cillian's body simmered with fury, and his eyes darkened as he looked right at me. "Abso-fucking-lutely not. I don't care if you being bonded to him saved a thousand lives. You're mine. Not his."

I couldn't stop myself from smiling at his outrage. Not that there was anything funny about our situation, but knowing how strongly he cared for me brought a much-needed happiness into my heart.

I leaned my head against his shoulder as we sat in his makeshift bed, leaning against the wall inside the cave. "I'm more than okay with that. I just wanted to make sure I wasn't being selfish by not sharing the thought once I'd had it."

His grip squeezed my hand tighter. "There is nothing selfish when it comes to us being together. I don't give a fuck what anyone else thinks."

My eyes fluttered closed, and I let my body relax against

Cillian's. It had been more than a week since I'd had decent sleep. While resting on the ground wasn't ideal, it was so much better than the nights I'd spent in that cell, alone with no light.

Cillian's fingers stroked over my cheek, and he kissed the top of my head. "Sleep, Mate. I'll wake you if there are any changes."

I nodded and burrowed in closer, sliding down until my head lay in his lap and my legs were curled up next to him.

The last thought I remembered before passing out was that nothing had ever felt safer than falling asleep with Cillian watching over me.

Something or someone was touching me, but I couldn't find the will to care. My body was warm, my eyes were heavy, and my mind was blank. I felt completely blissful.

For a short time, I'd forgotten where I was, what had happened, and what was to come. All I knew was that I was with Cillian and, for the moment, everything was okay.

"I need to go see Lykem," my mate's voice whispered into my ear. "I'll be back as soon as I can."

His hand brushed my hair back, and he started to move out from under me, but it was too late. I was awake, and everything from the day—hell, the week—before came flooding back.

I sat up and reached a hand up to him. "I'll go with you."

"You should keep sleeping," he said, but still pulled me up and held me against his chest.

"I should be wherever you are." The words sounded cheesy to my ear but felt right to my heart.

He nodded against my head. "Let's go then."

With our fingers connected, we walked back down the tunnels. Cillian's small section of space was in a corner with just four other people. I assumed it was the middle of the night, so I kept quiet as we traveled through the dark walkways.

Fire torches hung every twenty-or-so feet, casting just enough light for us to see where we were going, but I'd already forgotten which way was the exit. Thankfully, Cillian knew exactly where he was going.

We didn't pass any other shifters inside the cave, but once we were outside—where the moon was high in the sky and stars shined everywhere I looked up—I sensed several others nearby.

Lykem had been brought closer to the entrance of the cave and was still in his dragon form. From the conversations I'd heard earlier, that wasn't a good thing.

Standing next to him were Winter and two men I'd yet to meet. The nearest man had burns on the right side of his face that started at his forehead and continued down past the neckline of his shirt. He was the first to look over at us, his bright-green eyes landing on me, then Cillian.

"Fane," Cillian said to him, reaching a hand out. "Any updates?"

He shrugged, glancing over at the fallen dragon. "His heart beats steadily."

The other man stepped forward, this one several inches

shorter than both Cillian and Fane, but wide set with muscles on top of muscles. His auburn hair fell over his forehead when he nodded in agreement. "The longer he lives, even in this form, the higher chance we'll see him make a full recovery. All of his bones reset as they needed to."

Cillian grimaced. "Rebreaking his wing wasn't the most fun thing I've ever done."

"But it was necessary," Fane said.

I left Cillian's side and went to Lykem's prone dragon. His wings were folded perfectly over his sides, and he was laying on his belly with his neck and head folded inward.

My eyes met Winter's. "His stomach is already healed enough to lay on it?"

She nodded, her fair skin glowing under the moon above us. "All of his wounds are."

"Then what is keeping him unconscious?" I asked, not understanding how their abilities worked.

"Could be a number of things." She shrugged. "The sheer trauma of the situation. His dragon needing more rest before being able to shift again. He also could just be exhausted and doesn't want to wake up."

I half snorted and laughed. It wasn't as if I knew Lykem well, but that last one seemed more than possible.

I kneeled next to him and placed my hand on his head. "Rest all you need, Dragon Boy. Just make sure to wake up soon enough."

His scales were cool to the touch, whereas they'd been warm when he'd first arrived, which was good. Though, his scales didn't flinch or quiver as I pet him like I hoped.

Deciding not to disturb him any further, I stood back up and glanced over at Cillian. "What time is it?"

"About four in the morning."

"Is time ahead or behind or the same as back home?" I asked, realizing I hadn't even considered if time moved differently in this realm. Though, he'd compared it to Fae Islands, so I doubted that was a concern I needed to stress over.

"We're three hours ahead of the academy," he answered. "Not sure what that means for your home."

Shit. If we were ahead, then it was still the middle of the night for Beatrix and even my parents in Texas.

My skin itched, though, and my chest felt tight.

I've been...what would you call it? my wolf pondered. *Meditating. Figuring out this extra energy is key, but you're reacting because we need to get back to Earth, regardless of the time*, she confirmed.

Any idea why?

It's just time.

Well, that wasn't cryptic as fuck or anything.

I stepped closer to Cillian and grabbed his hand again. "I'd like to head back now if there's nothing else we can do for Lykem."

"Now?" he asked, and I nodded. "Okay."

That was easier than I expected. Then again, not really.

He turned to the others. "I'm not sure when we'll be back. It could be a few hours or even a couple days, but we'll do our best to make the trip quick."

The man whose name I didn't catch earlier nodded. "We've already been discussing ways to retaliate now that we know where he's hiding, thanks to your mate. We'll be ready to act when you're back."

"Thanks, Clay," Cillian said. "So will we."

I remembered something I wanted to make sure they knew as well. "According to Knox, he's the only one who can open the door into his underground bunker, but I was able to leave on my own. Something to keep in mind."

"We're working on our cloaking spells and hoping to ambush him when he comes out to attack us," Clay said. "But good to know we'll be able to get out on our own once we're inside. Our first goal will be to get Darius back, so that Knox can't use his scales any longer."

Fuck. I'd completely forgotten about Cillian's father. When I glanced up at my mate and found tension around his eyes, it was clear he hadn't.

"We'll hurry back," I said with certainty. There was no way that our time with my family would be the reason Cillian missed the raid to rescue his father. Plus, there was also his Nannio to concern ourselves with.

Though, I wasn't going to bring up that sore subject until we were back.

I glanced around the sky. "Do you think it's safe for my wolf to run to the portal?"

As much as I needed to shift, I wasn't going to put anyone else in danger to do so.

He nodded. "There are other dragons still out there, flying around to keep watch. I'll shift and make sure they know what we're doing."

My hands reached up, and I grabbed his face, bringing him closer to me. "We're going to be okay."

His jaw was still riddled with tension. "I know."

I didn't believe that he did know, but I let it slide. I might have been captured and forced to bond with his brother, but Cillian had lost his mate, found out his grandmother was a traitor, came home to his world burning, and then nearly lost his oldest friend.

He could have this moment of despair.

You're ready to run, I assume? I asked my wolf.

More than.

As soon as Cillian had taken two steps away, I let the shift come over me. Energy simmered deep inside my bones and through my veins.

We're stronger, I pointed out.

We are. We're tapping into new energy here.

Like Luna Marked energy?

We briefly discussed this before, but she'd said it was different. Though, I didn't know where else we'd get more powers from if not the Moon Goddess.

Not Luna Marked, but it is a gift from our creator.

Well, at least I'd been on the right track with my thoughts.

She ended the conversation and trotted over to Cillian. Our head pressed against his stomach, and when his hands sank into our fur, a rumble of contentment echoed around us.

He bent down and pressed his head to ours. "It's nice to meet you under less stressful circumstances."

He really is perfect, my wolf cooed.

I wasn't surprised to see her swoon over him. She'd wanted this man the moment we'd sensed him.

Our wolf body wrapped around him, tail sliding across his back as we snuggled in.

The longer we stayed like this, the less tension I could sense from Cillian, but there was also a deeply rooted feeling of needing to run and get the hell out of there that I couldn't ignore for long.

We need to go, I reminded my wolf.

Before she backed away from him, she licked his face, making not only me laugh, but Cillian too.

"Time to run?" he asked, and we yipped in response. "I'll be right above you."

We waited until Cillian backed up and shifted. Once he was ready, all the energy we'd been forced to keep bundled up was pulsing along our skin and ready to burst free.

Run, I encouraged her, and without waiting another second, we were practically flying over the forest floor toward the portal.

Chapter Nineteen

CILLIAN

It was the middle of the night and freezing when we exited the portal into Earth. After making sure my renewed cloaking spell was fully intact, we stepped onto the icy snow. Dawsyn's nails dug into my arm when she almost slipped.

"And here I'd thought I was adjusting nicely to the cold after hanging around your mountain," she joked through a full-body shudder.

"We'll get you to the truck and be warmed up in no time," I said.

Her face twisted in a grimace. "What if your truck won't start? It's been sitting for a while. Hell, what if it's gone?"

Both things I hadn't considered, but there was only one way to know.

We walked carefully through the hardened snowpack and came around the corner. Right where I'd left it was the black truck I'd bought when I first got here after selling some enchanted stones from Drago to a local witch coven.

That had been a gamble, given the unique energy they'd contained, but we didn't have currency back home and I'd needed transportation.

I pulled my keys out that I'd thankfully remembered to grab before leaving to check on Lykem earlier. I'd known Dawsyn would be ready to go sooner rather than later.

The key fob still unlocked the truck, so the battery wasn't dead. That was a good start. I opened the driver's door and gestured for Dawsyn to slide over the bench seat. She stopped in the middle as I got in and quickly shut the door.

I reached between her legs and grabbed the charging cord, then pulled my cell phone from my jeans. It had died soon after coming back from talking to Dawsyn's parents last time, and I was sure they'd left plenty of messages for me.

After depositing the charging phone into the cupholder between Dawsyn's legs, I put the keys into the ignition, but all that happened when I twisted them was the sound of a struggling engine for two seconds before it died again. Given all the lights were on and the phone was charging, I knew it wasn't a battery issue.

I glanced at the gauges and snarled. "It's out of gas."

Someone must have drained the tank while it was sitting here, but I would have assumed they'd have broken in as well. Yet, nothing was touched.

"And it wasn't when you left it?" Dawsyn asked.

"No. At least a quarter tank was in there." My fist slammed against the steering wheel, and I tried to think of other solutions.

Dawsyn could shift into her wolf form and run in the

cold weather. I could tolerate walking and running as myself for quite a while in these temperatures, but it wasn't ideal.

Though, I wasn't sure what the point would be. The nearest gas station to here was close to an hour's drive, which would take a lot longer with me on two feet.

Just as I turned to look at Dawsyn and ask her what she thought we should do, a face appeared in the window on the passenger's side.

My entire body tensed, and I muttered a few choice words. "Your grandmother is starting to get on my last nerve."

Dawsyn grimaced. "She has a tendency to do that with everyone she meets."

She leaned over and opened the door. "Hello, GiGi."

Beatrix's eyes were locked on me. "Did you think I was going to leave you with an operational vehicle without proof that my granddaughter was okay?"

Now that she mentioned it...I wasn't the least bit surprised.

"Get out of the truck, and let's get out of these godforsaken mountains," Beatrix said, moving out of the way.

Dawsyn glanced over at me. "Are you okay going with her?"

Beatrix scoffed. "Is *he* okay? Shouldn't you be asking me if I'm okay, or even your parents? We all thought you were dead."

"It's fine," I said softly and got out of the truck.

She exited on my side, and we walked around the front of the truck to Beatrix who hadn't moved from the passenger's side. I met her hardened gaze. "I told you I would bring her back."

"What is your word worth to me yet?" she asked, this time without malice. "I don't know you. None of us do. Don't expect us to trust you with her so soon. You'll be disappointed otherwise."

Given how special I already knew Dawsyn was, I wasn't fazed by Beatrix's words. "Noted. Where do you want to take us?"

"Texas," she said with a groan. "Not my first choice, but Roman insisted you both came to the pack. They're probably sleeping, but I'm sure they won't mind being woken up."

The old witch should have been sleeping as well, but I didn't bother to tell her that.

She grabbed Dawsyn's wrist and then mine. Before I could ask what the hell she was doing, the ground fell out from underneath me, and my knees buckled in the next second.

Humidity smacked me in the face, and even though it was dark outside, I was already starting to sweat. Hell, this was worse than Drago.

My stomach churned as I righted myself before I could fall over. I'd never been teleported before and had only seen Beatrix use the portal. Something told me she'd purposely tried to throw me off balance.

"Doing okay there, dragon?" she asked, the left side of her mouth rising ever so slightly.

I was going to need to be more aware around this witch.

"Just fine." I glanced at Dawsyn, and she had her eyes closed. For a brief moment, I'd thought something was wrong, but her face was relaxed and there was a smile lifting at her lips.

I wanted to ask her what she was feeling, but I held my words back, waiting for her to come out of the moment.

When she looked at me, her golden eyes sparkled under the moonlight and her skin practically glowed. "Home. I didn't realize how much I'd missed my pack until I began to feel them all reappear within my mind."

"What do you mean?" I asked.

"Wolves are part of a pack," she said. "Everyone here is tied to my father as the alpha, and because of that shared connection, I sense each one of them when I'm close enough. Being as far away as I was at the academy, I'd lost that connection. At first, I'd been thankful, but now, I'm not sure how I thought I could live without it."

Hearing her words reminded me of one of the bigger obstacles we still faced. Being with Dawsyn wasn't going to be as easy as just *being* with her. We both had homes that we were deeply tied to. Homes that weren't in the same realm.

A woman with pinkish-purple hair came running toward us. She glared at me briefly, then smiled widely for Dawsyn.

I had a feeling this was going to be the way I was greeted for the foreseeable future. Hopefully, I could keep my thoughts about that to myself for my mate's benefit.

"Dawsyn," the woman murmured just before wrapping her arms around Dawsyn and picking her up off the ground.

Dawsyn hugged her back just as enthusiastically "Aunt Embry. I missed you."

"Missed you, too, kiddo." She finally put her down, then turned to me. "You must be Cillian."

I nodded. "Nice to meet you."

As she appraised me, I did the same to her. I may have wanted to keep my thoughts to myself, but that didn't mean my face couldn't say plenty.

She wore loose black pajama shorts and a dark-blue tank top with no shoes on. She must have been up and sensed Dawsyn's arrival. After hearing Dawsyn say she had a connection to all the pack members, I assumed they'd felt her return.

"You don't look like I expected," she said, her eyes softening toward me, then she turned back to Dawsyn. "You're okay?"

She nodded. "Thanks to him, I am."

"That's a lie," I cut in. "She escaped on her own. I only found her shortly afterwards."

Embry looped her arm through Dawsyn's. "Let's go inside the pack house and you can tell us all about these crazy-ass dragons."

Dawsyn went with her, but I stood, unsure if I should follow. Until Beatrix moved next to me, making me highly uncomfortable with her closeness.

"Wolf shifters thrive on their family," she said. "It's not normal how much they depend on each other. Don't feel too sorry for yourself when she chooses to ignore you."

Gods, this woman was a piece of work. Possibly even worse than my Nannio. Well, who I used to think she was.

When Dawsyn stepped onto the wraparound porch of the oversized white house, she finally turned. "Are you coming, Cillian?"

I smirked at Beatrix. "Seems you spoke too soon."

She didn't reply and didn't follow me as I walked toward my mate.

Embry was putting off a less hostile vibe as she led the way inside and took us to the left. We went down a hallway that was dark—as was most of the house this time of night —and ended up in a dining area.

She flicked on the lights and nodded up. "Want to go get them yourself or need me to do it?"

"I already talked to Mom," Dawsyn said. "They're getting dressed and coming downstairs."

I cocked my head to the side. "When did you talk to her?"

"Pack members can communicate telepathically," she said. "I thought dragons could do that as well."

"Only when we're shifted," I replied. "Unless we're blood family and then we can do it anytime, no matter the distance."

Dawsyn's eyes widened. "Can you contact Knox?"

It hadn't even occurred to me to try. "I don't know, and there's no reason to until he no longer has a tie to you. Antagonizing him before then doesn't seem like our best move, considering all the destruction he's caused."

What I wouldn't have given to tear him to shreds before when I'd had the chance. If Dawsyn hadn't been with me, I would have killed Knox without thinking twice. Instead, the bastard had nearly done the same to my oldest friend.

And I wouldn't soon forget.

Roman and Cait joined us, and I was surprised when Beatrix never followed. Unsurprisingly though, Dawsyn's parents ignored me while hugging their daughter and checking her over several times.

"What happened?" Cait asked, eyes wide but full of love for her daughter.

"Did you kill whoever took you?" Roman asked gruffly before Dawsyn could answer the first question.

Dawsyn squeezed both of their hands. "Why doesn't everyone sit down, and we'll explain."

The fact that she said "we'll" eased some of the tension in my chest. Tension I was sure wouldn't completely disappear until Knox was no longer a threat to my mate.

Roman's eyes landed on me, finally. "Thank you for bringing her home, where she belongs."

I wasn't sure how to respond to that because, at least for the time being, I'd felt Dawsyn had made it clear that she was going back to Drago with me.

Once everyone sat, Roman at the head of the table, Cait to his right, Dawsyn on the left with me next to her, and Embry across from me, Dawsyn spoke first.

"I'm glad to be here," she started. "But I first want to say that while coming back after those few weeks away has shown me things I hadn't been able to see before, it doesn't mean I'm staying."

Roman's hands curled into fists on top of the wooden table. "What do you mean? Where else would you go?"

"I have unfinished business in Drago, and I intend to see that through before deciding what the future holds for me." She kept her head up and stare strong as she spoke to her father.

They had a brief power struggle before Dawsyn looked

down. I had a feeling she'd only done that to ease the strain that was starting to drown the room.

"What is this unfinished business, sweetheart?" her mother asked. "Maybe we can help. Cillian said that we might be able to enter his realm, yes?"

I nodded. "Not at the moment, but we can change that again with some advanced notice."

Dawsyn squeezed my leg under the table, then began to recount all the events leading up to this moment, starting with her being taken from her dorm.

Her parents tried to interrupt her several times, but she held strong and finished everything before answering any questions.

By the time she was done, my rage was nearly uncontainable as I pictured her alone and starving in the cell Knox and Estelle had kept her in.

Part of me wished her wolf had ripped out my grandmother's throat on the way to freedom, so that I wouldn't need to face my traitorous grandmother. I was still undecided on how I was going to handle her when the time came.

It was hard to think that the same woman who had cared for me after I'd thought both my parents were dead was the same one working for Knox and who kept my mate locked away.

"So, you're still bonded to this man?" Cait asked first.

I suspected it was a question Roman wanted answered as well, but his jaw was wound so tight, I doubted he could speak at the moment.

"Yes," Dawsyn answered. "I'm hoping the two of you

know how to break a mate bond. If not, maybe GiGi can help?"

Cait frowned. "Beatrix couldn't help...out in a different situation. After a while, I just assumed it wasn't possible. Serene might also be a good person to ask. She's nearly senile now, but she still has her moments."

Embry scoffed. "She's been 'nearly senile' for a couple decades now. Let's ask Beatrix again. She may not have helped before, but that doesn't mean it was because she didn't know."

"But you're going to return back the pack after this Knox person is no longer an issue," Roman said, though it sounded more like a question even through his clenched jaw.

Dawsyn's hold on my leg increased. "I don't know, Dad."

"What do you mean?" he asked with a growl.

"I mean Cillian is my fated mate. The pack is my family. That will never change, but I can't promise this is where I will return."

Roman shoved his chair back, sending it tumbling over, then glanced briefly at his mate. "*This* is why I never wanted her to leave. I told you we'd lose her."

Chapter Twenty

DAWSYN

My father storming out of the dining room wasn't what I expected would happen. Did I think he was going to be happy that by finding my mate I might leave the pack and never return as an official member? Of course not, but I also didn't expect him to turn his back on me.

Mom also stood up, but she didn't leave the room. She came over to me and crouched until she could stare directly into my eyes. "He's only scared. Don't for one second think he's angry *with* you."

"I know." And I really did, but that didn't mean I was okay.

Mom turned her attention onto Cillian next. "What are you doing about the problems in your realm?"

"We'll be coordinating an attack now that we know where Knox is," he said. "But I told Dawsyn we had to come see you first since I'd promised to update you today and we also need to break the connection she has to him. He can track her, thanks to the bond."

She frowned and glanced at Embry. "Get Beatrix back in here."

"Already here," the witch in question said. "I was waiting for the worst of that conversation to be over. Didn't feel like hearing the alpha's pity party."

Nobody laughed except GiGi.

"Can you break the bond I have with the dragon shifter?" I asked her as she sat down in my father's recently vacated seat.

Her lips thinned, and she rolled her eyes. "Of course I can."

"Just like that?" Mom asked, a grin playing on her lips. "Of course you can? Why didn't I get the same answer when I asked all those years ago?"

"Because you didn't need my help. You needed to get your head right," GiGi lamented, then turned back to me. "You, on the other hand, don't belong with that lizard. We'll need to go to Spell House to break the bond, though."

I shouldn't have been surprised by that, even though I was disappointed. I knew getting back to Drago as soon as possible was important, but leaving without talking to my father wasn't going to sit right with me. I already felt that deep in my bones.

Give him until morning and he'll see things clearer, my wolf said. I hoped like hell she was right.

"What about this attack?" Aunt Embry asked. "How many people do you have fighting with you and how many will you be going up against?"

Cillian's mouth turned down slightly. "We don't know

how many Knox has with him, but we have at least thirty dragons who will fight with us."

My aunt shook her head and looked at Mom. "We need to go with them. Call the others. We can't let..."

The emotions choking at Aunt Embry made my throat tense and eyes burn.

"I'm going to be fine," I promised. "Knox might have kidnapped me, but that was before..." Yeah, I should have led with this part, but they could be mad about that later. "I learned I have Moon Goddess energy."

All four of them had their eyes on me. Though Cillian was already aware of this revelation, he likely didn't understand the importance of it.

"What do you mean?" Mom asked, moving back to her seat.

GiGi smirked. "She means that you passed on some of that moon juju to her."

That wasn't how I would have described it, but... "When I escaped from the underground tunnels I'd been kept in, my wolf shifted and as we ran for our lives, she glowed a silver color."

"I saw it with my own eyes," Cillian said. "She radiated power unlike any I've ever felt, and she was incredibly fast."

"Can you do anything different?" Mom asked, lines deepening around her eyes and mouth, still not seeming very happy with this news.

"Not that I'm aware of, but I do feel stronger and more capable," I said. "With Cillian and the others, I'm not afraid to go against Knox and whatever dragons he has with him. They won't be able to shift in the tunnels. As long as I stay in there, helping however I can, then there won't be nearly as much danger for me."

Aunt Embry drummed her fingers over the dining table. "You're sure they can't shift underground?"

"I mean, they literally could, but they'd be stuck instantly," I answered. "The hallways aren't wide or tall enough for the size of dragons I've seen so far."

GiGi raised a brow, looking at my mate with renewed interest. "Just how big are you?"

Before Cillian could respond, I cut in. "That's not the point of this conversation. I need you all to trust that we can handle this part, and if we can't, then we'll let you know. For now, I'm only here to make sure you know I'm alive, with my mate, and okay. Or at least I will be as soon as I'm no longer tied to Knox."

Three of the most important women in my life shared a look I didn't like. Then, it was GiGi who spoke the words I'd already been fearing.

"Your connection to Cillian may not come back just because the one with Knox goes away," she said.

I recalled the burning of the tether I'd felt to him. The sorrow and agony as it turned to ash, floating away too quickly for me to grasp on to the pieces.

I swallowed thickly and nodded, but before I could speak, my wolf reminded me of something.

Our spirits have a history, she said. *It doesn't matter that we broke the bond. There will be a way to fix it.*

I had no way to know if she was right or just speaking positively, but I chose to believe her and relayed that information.

Cillian grabbed my hand with wide eyes. "You can speak to your wolf?"

"You *can't* speak to your dragon?" I countered, having assumed he already knew this information, but also feeling slightly stupid that we hadn't discussed it yet. In our defense, a lot had been going on.

"I can feel his emotions and, after all these years, can usually sense what he wants, but there are never any verbal exchanges," he answered, voice still filled with awe. "We were really mated before?"

"Our animals were. My wolf is certain of that fact," I replied, offering him a smile.

"We'll have to talk more about that later," he said, nodding toward the others who were staring intently at us.

Right. My family was a bunch of nosey bastards. Still, I loved them with all my heart.

"It doesn't matter if you're not sure that our connection will come back," I said. "I know it will. I'd like to stay the rest of the night here and then head to Spell House in the morning. Then, we'll need to get back to Drago just as soon as the tie to Knox is cut."

"Is the fight happening that soon?" Mom asked, a crease between her brows.

"Possibly," Cillian answered. "But I also left behind a friend who was badly injured, and I'd like to make sure he's healing as he should be."

"One who was injured making sure Cillian could get me to safety," I added with a pointed stare at each of them.

"Fair enough," Aunt Embry said.

My mom's lips thinned and shoulders sagged. "Says the

one who doesn't have to convince her father of the same thing."

Embry grinned widely. "Just get naked and then tell him. It'll be fine."

It didn't matter that I was an adult and fully aware that they had sex. At no point in my life would it be okay for people to talk about it in front of me.

I stood up and pulled at Cillian's hand. "Well, that's enough for us. We're going to my room." I glanced at GiGi. "What time should we be ready?"

"I need to get back to my grumpy man and make sure he knows I haven't vanished on him." She chuckled. "I do that often. After appeasing him," her brows waggled, "I'll be back here around seven."

For fuck's sake. I also had no desire to hear about my grandmother's sex life.

Cillian laughed beside me as I groaned and waved a goodbye to my mom and aunt. I led him back down the hallway and to the stairs that went to the second floor where my room was.

He leaned forward and whispered in my ear. "You're adorable when you're embarrassed." His fingers brushed my cheek. "You get this blush that I want to see more often."

There were plenty of ways I could tell him how to make that "blush" appear more often, but that probably wasn't the best topic of conversation under the same roof as my father, who already wasn't happy with my life choices.

As we went up the steps to the second floor, I saw Cillian turn back. "What do those other stairs go to?"

"The pack library," I answered. "We can check that out if you'd like."

"I think I've spent enough time in one library over the past month to last me a lifetime," he muttered.

"And to think the book was never even there." I stopped, and he bumped into my back. "We never did ask Beatrix about the siphoning spell you asked her to work on."

He nodded and placed his hand on the small of my back. "I know. I'm not sure we actually need it now, but if she's willing to hand the potion over, then I'll gladly take it."

My head swiveled to look up at him. "What do you mean?"

"My grandmother had made me believe that there were larger forces at play this whole time," he said. "In reality, it was the two of them stealing power from other dragons and twisting that power into something they never should have had access to themselves. I don't need a spell to rip Knox's head from his neck."

I wanted to ask what his plans for Estelle were, but I knew that if it was Beatrix who had betrayed us, I wouldn't know what I'd be willing to do until I was forced. I'd have to decide in the moment.

For now, Cillian didn't need those kinds of thoughts circling inside his head.

Chapter Twenty-One

CILLIAN

Walking into Dawsyn's room, in a house that she shared with her parents and whoever else in the pack might sleep there, wasn't at all the same as bringing her into my home. Not that there was anything wrong with her still living with her parents—I'd gathered that was typical for a wolf pack—but still. I wasn't going to be touching her. Not when I already knew her father was pissed off about...everything.

"You've got to be shitting me?" she groaned.

I shook my head as I adjusted my pillow. "Not even a little bit."

"It's not like I'm going to seduce you. We're only going to get a few hours rest."

My brow raised. "You say that now. Just be thankful that I'm sleeping on the mattress."

"You mean on the comforter with all of your clothes still on," she grumbled.

Dawsyn was tucked in under the navy-blue blanket, and I was content right on top, with a foot of space between us.

"If your parents walk in—" I started to say, but she cut off.

"I'm a grown-ass woman. They know I've had sex." Her huff of annoyance was everything, even if the topic of conversation wasn't one I wanted to partake in. Hearing about her past sexual partners was something I never needed to know about. Not unless she wanted them dead.

"Go to sleep, Dawsyn."

She made a grunting noise, then rolled onto her side, back to me. "You're...not fun."

That might have been the case, but she'd just proved my point. If I'd have gotten ready for bed like I normally did, we wouldn't have gotten any sleep.

Not that I needed it.

I'd had a few hours back in the cave and that was more than I'd had in one go since Dawsyn had been taken.

Though, it wasn't long before the steady thrum of my mate's heartbeat and her soft breathing lulled me to sleep right next to her.

A short time later, the sun peeked through her sheer curtains, and I was the first one awake. I took a moment to take in her room with more light and noticed the wolf paintings on the wall, all of the same wolf that looked just like Dawsyn's. There was no signature on them, but they were stunning, and I wondered if she'd painted them herself.

She stirred next to me, and I leaned over, pulling her closer to my chest. "Good morning."

The smile she offered me nearly stopped my heart. "Morning."

I leaned down and kissed her softly. "Feel better sleeping in a real bed?"

I hated that I couldn't properly provide for her yet, but that would change. Just as soon as I ripped Knox's heart from his chest.

She shrugged. "I'd have felt better with your arms around me."

If only she knew how much I agreed with her.

Dawsyn slid out of the bed, wearing boy-short underwear and a white tank top. She stretched her arms toward the ceiling with her back to me and then...bent over.

I threw myself back onto the bed, stole her pillow to cover my face, and groaned loudly. "You're not nice."

"You started this. I'm just finishing it."

I'd done no such thing. All I'd tried to do was be a gentleman in her parents' home.

"I'm going to take a shower," she said, but I didn't take the pillow from my head until I heard the click of a door shutting.

Even then, I only pulled it back slowly.

I knew if I saw her naked body, I would cave. I'd carry her to the shower myself and have my face buried between her tits in a matter of seconds. Fuck. I wanted that so damn badly, but I also knew our situation was littered with tension. I wasn't going to make it worse.

I'd be taking a shower long after she was dressed and done with her room. In the meantime, I had to piss and needed to find another bathroom.

The mattress groaned beneath my weight as I stood up and headed toward the door. Just as soon as I opened it,

Roman was there with his fist in the air as if he was about to knock.

We openly stared at each other. Though, he was no longer wearing his emotions on his face and I had no clue what he was thinking.

"Dawsyn just got in the shower," I said, assuming he was looking for his daughter.

He glanced toward the bathroom door, then grinned as I heard Dawsyn yell, "Don't go with him!"

Before I could figure out what she meant, Roman grabbed my shoulder. "Let's go have a chat."

I should have seen that coming. He seemed rather attached to his daughter. Though, I didn't blame him. I hoped one day Dawsyn and I would have a little girl just like her. If I were a lucky enough bastard for that to happen, I knew I'd be the same way Roman was currently being.

Even though I knew Dawsyn wasn't happy about her father coming to get me, I went with him. She had to know there was no avoiding this.

He let go of my shoulder once I exited the bedroom and led me to another set of stairs at the end of the hallway. These went straight up and into an office.

"Have a seat." He pointed to one of the chairs in front of his desk as he walked around to take his own seat.

I sat with my back straight but shoulders relaxed. Did I want to get along with my mate's family? Of course, but I wasn't going to cower to anyone, either.

Dawsyn was mine, and there wasn't anything anyone could say or do to change that. Well, except Dawsyn.

I just hoped Roman could understand that.

He leaned back in his chair and steepled his fingers over

his lap, looking me right in the eyes. I felt his alpha power, but it didn't seem as if he was trying to challenge me, so I kept his stare.

"I was lucky when I found my Cait," he began. "She didn't have any family and her best friend already belonged to my pack. There were still some obstacles, but this was where she was always meant to be. Right here in East Texas with me and the pack."

He paused, but I kept quiet. I had a feeling I knew where he was going, but I wasn't going to help him get there.

"When Dawsyn was born, I'd never been more terrified in my life," he continued. "She was this tiny little thing, and I was responsible for keeping her alive. It was my job to protect her and provide for her. To make sure she knew how to handle whatever life might throw at her. She's *my* little girl."

Only she isn't so little anymore, I thought.

He cleared his throat. "Never did I think I had to prepare for her finding a mate in a dragon or that by doing so, she'd be put right in the middle of a battle she shouldn't be fighting."

"I never asked Dawsyn to fight," I said. "In fact, I'd rather she not, but your daughter isn't the type to be told what to do."

His laugh was strangled. "She's more like her mother than I hoped she'd be, but at the same time, she's so much more than I could have wished for." He paused and glanced out the window. "I understand that you two had a mate bond, and I know you're aware of the ramifications from your brother—"

"He's no brother of mine," I interjected sharply.

Roman's eyes pinched at the sides briefly, but he continued. "From the forced bond she took to save River. I also know by looking at my daughter and seeing the way she watches you that it doesn't matter if that bond returns or not. You're still her fated mate."

I fucking hoped so. "And she's mine. There isn't anything I wouldn't do for her."

He raised both brows. "*Anything*?"

"Anything that she asks of me," I specified. If Dawsyn told me she wanted to stay here at her pack after Knox was dealt with, then that was what we'd do, but only if that was what she wanted. Not because her father made us feel like it was what we should do.

I had no doubts Dawsyn loved her pack, but she'd left for a reason, and I wasn't going to force her to return.

"Very well," he said. "Her mother and I have spoken, and we support whatever Dawsyn wants to do. I just need you to know that sometimes what our mates want isn't always the best choice. I need to know that if she's putting herself in danger, you're not going to be afraid to step in and stop her."

"You mean, regardless of how much she might hate me in the moment, there may come a time when I have to force her to sit out of the fight?"

He grinned. "Precisely. I've done it for my mate and don't regret that choice to this day."

"I will always put the safety of Dawsyn above all else," I said, leaving it at that. Promising to control my mate wasn't something I could do. Not to her.

Though, that didn't mean I wouldn't if there were no other choice.

"That's all I can ask for." He stood and I did the same, but before I could say anything else, he added, "Well, that's not exactly true. I'd love to ask for the two of you to stay here, but my mate said I wasn't allowed to do that."

I grinned. "I hear you, but I'm not the one you should be *not* asking."

Where we lived would be up to Dawsyn. If she chose here, then I'd have to figure out what to do about my dragon, but as long as we were with our mate, then I knew he wouldn't mind staying hidden if that was necessary.

"Let's go downstairs, so my daughter and mate can quit yelling at me." He gestured toward the door and I headed back into the hallway ahead of him.

"Makes me a little more thankful that dragons can't communicate the same way," I said.

Roman shrugged. "It's more of a benefit than anything else most days."

As we headed toward the other set of stairs, he glanced at me again. "Thank you for bringing her back to us."

"I would have looked for her until I died."

"And that's the only reason I don't want to kill you right now." His face was devoid of any emotion, and he brushed past me without another word.

So much for thinking our chat had been more of a positive one.

Chapter Twenty-Two

DAWSYN

My mother had tried to distract me by having my aunts and their mates over to say a quick hello and goodbye to me, but nothing could make my mind stop wondering what the hell my father and mate were talking about upstairs.

When Dad's voice had sounded in my mind and told me that he was borrowing Cillian, I almost ran naked out of the shower to stop them but decided better of it.

I drummed my fingers on the table over and over until Beatrix finally smacked my hand. "Quit your fussing. Your father won't hurt him, and I've been watching Cillian. Unfortunately, he's impressed me. It seems that boy would do anything for you, and I'm sure that includes listening to Roman toss idle threats at him."

That had a smile lifting on my face. Cillian was the perfect mix of sweet and strong. I knew he could burn the world if he wanted, but he also cared deeply about many different things. Most important being me.

Knowing that had been one of the things keeping me calm lately.

Footfalls sounded in the hallway, and it was my father who appeared first. Alone.

"Where's Cillian?" I asked, standing up and looking behind him.

"He's coming." Dad went to Mom, wrapped his arm around her waist, and pressed his lips to the side of her head. Even after all these years, he couldn't enter a room without touching her first.

Ten seconds later, Cillian walked into the kitchen. I gave him a onceover, and he seemed fine. Not angry or annoyed or anything in between.

I was nice, my dad's voice sounded in my head.

You've given me no reason to believe that without Cillian confirming so.

I glanced back at him, and my father grinned. He knew what he'd been doing and was proud of it.

My fingers laced through Cillian's, and I looked up at him. "Did you want to take a shower before we go?"

He cringed a little. "Probably should."

"I'm sure we have some clothes you can have, too," Mom offered, stepping away from my reluctant father.

She pulled my mate away from me, and just like that, he was now alone with my other parent. This was just such a great morning.

"We leave in five minutes," GiGi said loud enough that I knew my mother and Cillian would have heard her, then she huffed. "I'm going to go wait outside. I don't need to be present for whatever gush fest the two of you are about to have."

I'd had no intentions of doing that with my father now, but when I looked at him again, his eyes were much softer than they'd been since I'd returned home.

As soon as Beatrix went out the back door of the kitchen, Dad came over to me and grabbed my hand before gesturing for us to sit at the table together.

"I'm sorry that I didn't handle last night as well as I should have," he said first, surprising me. I was pretty sure the only person I'd ever heard him apologize to was my mother.

I didn't reply immediately, because telling him it was okay to turn his back on me didn't sit right in my chest.

"You've never walked away from me before," I said instead.

His eyes cast down. "I know, and I knew it was wrong as soon as I'd taken my first step in the opposite direction, but I let fear continue to push me away. Since the moment you were born, there's been nothing I've wanted more than to keep you safe."

I squeezed his hand. "You can't do that forever, Dad."

"I know. I also know that you've grown up to be an incredible woman, and I've kept you too close for too long now," he admitted.

"But you also taught me how to protect myself and be smart in all sorts of situations."

He finally grinned again. "You always were an excellent fighter during trainings. You know, people haven't always treated you differently because you're the alpha's daughter or because you have the alpha gene. You're powerful in your own right, Dawsyn. Nothing I taught you can take away from that. I'm sorry if I didn't make you see that truth before, but I hope you feel it now."

I had thought I was already feeling his words, but it wasn't until I heard them leave his mouth that I felt my chest rise and shoulders push back.

All my life I'd wanted to be something more, and I never thought I could be until I left home. I briefly thought that if only I'd known... Yet, the path I'd taken and the feelings I'd had, they'd all led me to Cillian. I couldn't have any regrets about that.

I leaned forward and wrapped my arms around my father's neck. "Thank you, Dad. For everything. Even all the things I didn't realize at the time that you were doing for me."

His hands pressed against my back, and he rested his head against mine. "Always, baby girl. No matter how old you get, where you live, or what you do, I'm always here for you."

I pulled back enough that I could see his face, keeping my hands on his shoulders. "Even if I'm in a different realm."

"Even then," he promised, then winked. "Doesn't mean I'll be happy about it, but I'll get over it. Your mother will make sure of that."

I chuckled. "She always does."

"Who always does what?" Mom asked as she strutted into the kitchen as if she hadn't been standing in the hallway listening for most of that conversation.

"Oh, nothing," Dad said.

My cheeks began to hurt, and my heart was fuller than it had been in far too long. Everything was nearly perfect, aside from the dark spot in my chest where the connection to Knox still festered inside me.

My mom walked around the smaller kitchen table and came up behind me, hugging me from behind. "You're an incredible woman, and you've found yourself a rather respectful mate."

I wanted to grumble that he was a little too respectful, but I didn't think my father would appreciate that.

"Thanks, Mom." My head leaned back against her shoulder, and my hands were still entwined with my dad's. We stayed like that, quiet in each other's company, just soaking up the warmth of our little family until Cillian came back downstairs.

When he entered the kitchen, he came to an abrupt stop, then backed up until I called for him.

"I didn't mean to interrupt," he said, freshly showered, wearing fresh jeans and a new light-grey shirt. He smelled as if he needed to be licked from head to toe.

My heart began to race, and I had to let go of my dad's hands because...just no. I stood up from the chair and I nodded toward the back yard. "We should go before Beatrix leaves without us."

Mom made an awkward noise from behind. Awkward for me, at least. I had no doubts that she knew why I was eager to leave.

Cillian stepped toward me, but then turned to my father and shook his hand. "Thank you for letting me stay in your pack and trusting me with your daughter."

Fuck, he really was respectful. I was merely ready to bolt and there was my mate, making nice with my parents.

Dad nodded. "That trust only lasts until she gets hurt."

I rolled my eyes and turned to say goodbye to Mom whose arms were already open and waiting for me. "Be safe and trust your instincts. We don't know what that extra boost of power you had is from. I wish we had more time to figure it out, but I understand that you don't. Just be careful."

"Always." I hugged her tightly, then turned to my dad before things could get too emotional.

His embrace was quick as well, but he held tightly to my biceps and kept me close a beat longer. "You know who you are, Dawsyn. Never forget that."

A heaviness settled over me, and I nodded. I may not have known all the words to explain who I was, but in my heart, I agreed with him.

I was Dawsyn Chase. The daughter of two alpha wolves and the mate of a dragon, but more than those things, I was...something powerful. I'd sensed that for a long time now and it was why I'd wanted to know if there had ever been Luna Marked children before. I'd thought that I needed to figure out what that something was to feel whole, but coming home made me realize that wasn't the case.

I needed to believe in myself and know that I was capable of so much more than I'd yet to realize, but I would when the time was right.

Cillian was already at the back door by the time I pulled away from my father and I took another, longer look at him. I had no idea where the clothes had come from, because my mate was taller and broader than my dad, but damn, I still wanted to lick him.

The tips of his still-wet hair hung over his forehead, and

his skin glowed. Though, not as bright as it did back home where he didn't have to conceal his dragon.

The shirt fit snugly across his chest, and the jeans made me want to pinch his ass cheeks.

I shook my head, once again wondering how the hell I resisted him for those first couple of weeks.

Temporary insanity is my vote, my wolf chimed.

You don't get a vote, I said as I walked out the door with Cillian, a grin on my face.

I sensed my wolf's disagreement, but she went back to her meditating, which I was okay with. Breaks from having a voice in my head were sometimes nice, and figuring out what our extra strengths were would be helpful before we got back to Drago.

"About damn time," Beatrix grumbled with her back to us as she began to open a portal. "Let's go."

I glanced up at Cillian to find him smiling at me. "Ready?" he asked.

"More than."

GiGi snorted, then just as we stepped through the portal into the attic of Spell House, she added, "You say that now, but soon you'll be begging me for a merciful death."

"Beatrix!" My father's bellow was the last thing I heard before she followed us through and closed the opening.

Chapter Twenty-Three

DAWSYN

Cillian's chest was rumbling as he stood ramrod straight next to me. "What did you mean by that?"

GiGi smirked. "If you thought breaking a bond was going to be a joyride, you're not as smart as I thought you were. I'll literally be ripping her soul apart, thanks to those dragon scales of yours."

"My soul?" I swallowed thickly.

She nodded and headed toward a table where there were stacks of books. "I've been doing research and, while there is nothing that specifically mentions dragons, I know how to read between the lines. Plus, with the scales and blood I already had, it was easy to piece everything together. I can unfortunately understand why the dragons have remained hidden for so long."

"So, this isn't just magic that needs to be broken?" I asked. "Knox isn't my fated mate. How can he be tied to my soul?"

"Because dragons have unique energy, which you stupidly absorbed and made worse by being in Drago for as long as you were." She snapped her fingers and looked back up at me. "Speaking of which, River is going to murder you if you don't call him soon."

"I don't have my phone and haven't had access to one," I explained. Though, it wasn't necessary. She didn't care.

"We'll start with you sitting in that chair over there," GiGi said to me, then pointed to Cillian. "Move those large crystals so that they'll be in a circle around Dawsyn."

She went back to reading, and my eyes met Cillian's. There was a deep crease between his brows and his lips were pressed thin. "You don't have to do this. We can kill him and that will solve the problem."

GiGi tsked from across the room. "Not true. If Knox dies, his spirit will still be tied to her until she dies. Your chances of reigniting your fated mate bond are already low. They'll be nonexistent if she doesn't do this before the lizard is dead."

My palms pressed against Cillian's chest, and I smiled. "It's okay. It will be a temporary pain for an even larger reward."

"I hate that I couldn't save you from this," he muttered quietly.

"You'll need to be okay with not always saving me," I said. "I'm an alpha at heart. There isn't much I'll back down from, especially when it means saving the lives of others."

"The one thing I equally admire and hate about you." His lips briefly twisted into a smirk. Just as he was getting ready to lean in for a kiss, Beatrix snapped her fingers again.

"We don't have all day, children. Don't waste my time."

All I could do was smile. I knew my GiGi loved me

more than the sun and moon, and her curt attitude only proved that more. She was nervous. Nothing made her crankier than that.

Cillian headed toward the group of crystals in the cabinet behind Beatrix while I found my way to the wooden chair at the center of the attic space.

Shelves filled with ancient books lined the wall to my right, and there was a window with stained glass in front of me. The wood floors creaked with every step Cillian took, and Beatrix hummed behind me, where I assumed she still stood with her books and potions on the table.

There was a house full of witches and warlocks below us, but with the magically sealed door that led to the rest of the house, they were none the wiser that we were up here. Unless one of the higher-ranking witches decided to come up.

Though, I had a feeling my grandmother had purposely made sure they'd be busy elsewhere before bringing us to the attic. She liked her secrets, and it was no fun for her when someone ruined them.

Cillian finished placing the clear crystal pillars around my chair. I thought he was going to come over to me, but I heard him approach Beatrix instead. I turned out of curiosity and heard him ask about something I'd forgotten about.

"Do you have the siphon spell here?"

She glanced up from the bowl of ingredients she was mixing. "Why?"

"I don't think I'll need it now that I know who we're dealing with, but if you have the potion ready, it might not hurt to have," he replied, leaning lightly against the tall table.

GiGi grinned. "I lied before. The spell calls for the leaf of a plant that doesn't seem to be grown any longer, and considering my granddaughter was missing, I haven't exactly been focusing on other things. Though, I had no problem letting you think I had what you needed."

Cillian didn't seem the least bit surprised by that revelation, and neither was I. He walked toward me instead of replying back to her. A smart choice, because my grandmother seemed to be in more of a mood than normal, thanks to the complexity of my situation.

"You're sure we won't need the spell still?" I asked when he kneeled next to me, placing his hands on my thighs.

His shrug was slight. "The grandmother I now know I can't trust was the one who told me it was what we needed. Maybe she knew it was going to be impossible to get and merely wanted me out of the way."

He made a valid point. "So, you think we free your father and kill Knox, then all of this will be over?"

"That's the plan until someone does something that decides otherwise," he said, looking up at me with a tense jaw. "I don't know what I'm going to do about my grandmother, though."

"I'll gladly handle her for you," my GiGi said, making me inwardly grin. Seeing the two of them battle would be quite the sight.

I may not have known Cillian's grandmother, but by the short moments I did spend with her and the things I'd heard Cillian say about her before, I had little doubt that it would be one hell of a showdown.

GiGi bumped her hip into Cillian's back. "You're going to want to leave this circle unless you want to suffer irreversible consequences."

He didn't bother to look back at her. His stare stayed with mine as he rose far enough up that his forehead pressed against mine. "You're going to be okay."

The words were said with a fierce intensity and penetrated right into my chest, but I also knew they were said for his benefit as much as mine.

I nodded and offered him a smile. "I am. Beatrix won't let anything happen to me."

"Not anything that you can't heal from," she muttered, making Cillian's lip lift into a snarl.

My hands squeezed around his face. "I'm in the most capable hands for the job. Even if she has shitty bedside manner. I promise."

"You better be right." His mouth pressed against mine, staying in place for longer than I expected. The kiss never deepened, but just feeling his warmth, allowing it to soak into me, was all I needed in that moment.

He pulled, or more accurately, was pulled away from me, eliciting a growl from both of us.

"Don't go feral on me now," GiGi said. "The longer you drag this out, the more it's going to hurt."

That was likely a lie, but I let her have it.

I squeezed Cillian's hand, and he kissed the top of my head before walking out of the circle.

My eyes closed, and I called out to my wolf. *I hope all the meditating you've been doing is about to do us some good right now.*

Not likely, but one can hope, she replied. *Don't worry. I'm right here with you.*

She didn't really have a choice in the matter, but I appreciated her words, nonetheless.

Beatrix pulled rope from her pockets and started to tie my hands to the chair without saying a word.

"Care to explain what you're doing?" I asked.

"I'm making sure you don't punch me and ruin the whole thing," she deadpanned.

I shook my head. "Might want to tie my legs, too. Wouldn't want me to kick you, either."

While I was being incredibly sarcastic because I had faith in my self-control, she seemed to take me very seriously and bent to one knee.

"Do you really think those are going to hold me?" They were thin, maybe a half-inch thick and made from what I assumed to be cotton.

"If I'd just brought them home from the store, no," she said. "But these have been upgraded. Shifter and vampire proof." Then, she waggled her brows. "Even sorcerer proof."

I gagged and squeezed my eyes closed. "GiGi, I do *not* need to know about your extracurricular activities."

"Then, you shouldn't have asked," she quipped.

As soon as she tied the last knot, she reached into the bowl I'd seen on the table and flicked some sort of rancid concoction into my face.

I squeezed my eyes closed and coughed as my head shook. "Seriously, GiGi."

She didn't say anything else. Instead, something warm poured over my head and I kept my eyes sealed shut.

My fingers curled over the arm of the chair, nails digging into the wood. I tried not to breathe in the stench, but that was nearly impossible as my heart rate sped up.

I wanted to ask what the hell was happening, but goo slid down my face and there was no way I was opening my mouth for any reason.

"This might pinch a little," she warned right before her palm slammed over my heart.

My back arched, forcing my chest to push against her hand that I was nearly certain was burning through my skin.

The festering black hole of a connection that I had to Knox flared to life. It grew stronger inside me, expanding until I was certain it was going to swallow me whole.

Whatever shit Beatrix had poured onto me started to burn into my pores, and I swore it was entering my bloodstream and lighting a fire inside my veins.

She finally removed her hand from my chest. "He's stronger than I anticipated."

I badly wanted to ask what the hell she meant by that, but before I could chance opening my mouth, an electric current felt as if it was being stabbed through my skull then shooting down my spine.

A partial shift started, and my nails turned to claws, while I was certain fur had sprouted along my skin. My teeth elongated, and there was no keeping my lips together any longer.

As soon as the wretched sludge entered my mouth, I was convinced I'd throw up, but with the current of electricity still pulsing through me, I had no control over my body.

Dawsyn.

My name was a whisper of rage through my mind.

What the hell was that? I asked my wolf.

Knox. He's trying to connect deeper with you.

Fuck that nonsense.

"Get this bastard out of me," I yelled. Or at least, I think I did. There was a pounding inside my head that made me unsure of my volume.

I sensed my grandmother moving faster around me. I'd have expected her to answer, but there was no response. Or maybe I just couldn't hear it.

Either way, whatever she was doing next didn't seem to be helping.

The rope tied around my arms and legs was beginning to cut into my skin as my body tried desperately to get free of the restraints, only it wasn't me that wanted free. I wasn't controlling my movements.

The spell Beatrix used must have opened the connection between the two of you further, my wolf said. *It's as if his spirit is right here with us, fighting against whatever she's doing.*

Based on the conflicting actions of my body, I could believe that, but I didn't understand why. Knox had hardly paid attention to me while I'd been in his possession. Did he truly hate his brother enough that he just didn't want Cillian to have me?

I didn't know for sure, and a part of me hoped I never found out. That the fucker would be nothing more than a corpse the next time I saw him.

There was a pulsing sensation inside my chest, and my hands wanted nothing more than to sink my claws through my skin and rip my own heart out. The desire wasn't mine, but it felt so fucking tangible that I could taste the fury inside my mouth.

My eyes finally opened, wider than I thought should have been possible. My head jerked back, then slammed forward over and over again.

"Stay still, damn it," GiGi demanded, but it wasn't me. I'd lost control of my own body.

"Can't...stop...him." My words were garbled, but I got them out right before the pounding in my head intensified so severely that all I could hear was the sound of an invisible windstorm circling my body.

Dawsyn.

Knox's faint voice echoed through the cyclone, but I ignored him and focused on Cillian. The bond I'd had with my true mate, while never completed, had ignited a warmth inside me that I'd never felt before. Something I knew I would never feel again with anyone other than him.

Cillian's strength and resilience were all I needed to keep me grounded in this moment. It didn't matter that our tether had been turned to ash. I could still imagine the power of knowing he was mine. Even if I'd wanted to reject him at first, a part of my heart had always known.

He was ours.

Not Knox. Not anyone else.

It would only ever be Cillian.

His brother was an unwanted houseguest who needed to get the fuck out of my mind and heart.

With a roar that started deep in my stomach and grew with every inch it rose through my body, I snarled and yelled, using the drive inside me to fuel whatever my grandmother was doing.

My body vibrated with energy, and with every beat of my heart and scorching pulse in my veins, I felt Knox getting further and further away.

You're going to regret this, he taunted faintly. *I will kill them all.*

The howl in my mind turned into a growl that reverberated through my chest until the heat left my body and I had control again.

A bucket of water was poured over my head, and then the ropes were cut from my bruising skin. I swiped my hands over my eyes, then turned toward a magically restrained and very pissed-the-fuck-off-looking Cillian and Beatrix.

"We need to go," I snarled. "Now."

Chapter Twenty-Four

CILLIAN

Watching Dawsyn be stripped of the bond felt like someone had been cutting my heart out with a dull blade. When I couldn't take her screams any longer, I'd lunged for my mate, wanting to do anything I could to help ease her agony, but Beatrix had been prepared for that.

Her magic had wrapped around my body like a rope, locking me into place, then somehow silenced my voice. I'd stood there helpless to do anything, my ire growing with every rapid beat of my heart. I had no clue how much time had passed, but it was like an eternity in hell, knowing there was nothing I could do to stop whatever was happening to Dawsyn.

The longer I'd had to stand there trapped, the more hate I began to feel for *my* grandmother, not the one who had restrained me. Estelle had been the only one who had suspected I'd met a woman while I was at the academy. She must have told Knox. *She* was the reason my mate was suffering.

I thought I'd known Estelle or at least understood her,

but it seemed as if everything had been a lie. All these years of her caring for me... She'd merely been passing the time. But that was the least of my worries at the moment.

The green shit that Beatrix had poured over Dawsyn turned into smoke as soon as she dumped the bucket of water over my mate's head. Then, Dawsyn's vengeful eyes turned to us, and I knew something had gone wrong.

"We need to go," she practically growled. "Now."

Beatrix snapped her fingers, and the hold on my body was released. "You'd thank me if you understood the pain I just saved you both from by forcing you to stay put, but I won't be offended by your lack of gratitude."

I ignored the witch. I wasn't angry or grateful for her. I just needed my hands on Dawsyn. I was at her side before she even had the chance to stand all the way up. "What happened?"

"Knox was in my head," she said with a shudder. "I could hear his voice, faint yet clear. He wants to kill everyone because I broke the bond. We need to warn them." She turned to Beatrix. "Can you get us back to the portal?"

I glanced at Beatrix, waiting for her answer, and noticed dark circles starting to form under her eyes. She might have been a powerful sorceress, but even she couldn't hide her true age when she used the amount of magic that I suspected she'd just needed to.

"Do I look like a damn taxi to you?" she snarked, then walked over to the table she'd been at before, a slight wobble to her steps.

She lifted a stone cup to her lips and closed her eyes as she drank whatever was inside.

A visible shimmer started around her head and moved its way down her body. When I glanced back at her face, the dark circles were gone, but the lines and creases were still prominent.

The old witch rubbed her palms together and stepped around the table before thrusting them forward.

A silver circle formed, and a portal opened, but much slower than it had when she'd brought us here. As it opened, Beatrix turned to Dawsyn and waved a hand in her direction.

"That was more appreciated than you know, GiGi," Dawsyn said, and I realized Beatrix had used magic to dry my mate's clothes and clean up the mess they'd made.

"I felt the new energy inside you," Beatrix replied. "Be careful with that until you know how to control yourself. Power like that can just as easily strike you down as it can save your life."

"I won't use it unless I have to," Dawsyn said, then strode to my side and grabbed my hand with a tight smile on her face. "Are you ready?"

"I'd rather stay here and make sure that *you're* ready," I replied honestly.

She could walk and stand, but I'd heard her screams, felt them deep into my bones.

She'd just gone to hell and back, and now we were likely headed into a battle. I wasn't sure if she was ready for this, which made Roman's previous words filter back through my mind.

"I need to know that if she's putting herself in danger, you're not going to be afraid to step in and stop her."

I didn't want to control Dawsyn, but I also wouldn't be

able to live with myself if she died because I didn't make sure she was rested and prepared to fight.

Her fingers rubbed over her chest, and I watched the movements, realizing that she never confirmed if Beatrix's spell had worked.

"Is the bond gone?" I asked, my voice barely a whisper.

While I fucking hoped so, a small part of me wished she'd say no, because where our bond should have reignited, there was nothing other than a whisper of a memory of what used to be.

She nodded stiffly, eyes casting downward.

I lifted her chin with one hand and stared deep into her eyes. "Bond or not, you're mine, Dawsyn Chase."

I meant the words with every fiber of my being, and I hoped she knew that. Nothing else mattered to me any longer. From the moment I saw her in that shower back at the academy, she was all I needed in my life.

Beatrix cleared her throat. "It's cold enough to freeze nipples out here, and I'd like to go drink my weight in whiskey after all that. So, if you wouldn't mind...get the hell out."

A grin played on Dawsyn's lips, and she squeezed my hand before stepping toward her grandmother. She embraced the elder witch, then lightly kissed her cheek. "Thank you, GiGi. For everything."

Her eyes softened, and there might have even been a shimmer of tears there before she blinked. "Yeah, just try not to need that kind of help again, okay?"

Dawsyn laughed. "I'll do my best."

I gave Beatrix a curt nod. Something told me she didn't need or want my gratitude.

Together, Dawsyn and I stepped through the portal that led back to the mountain in Montana. Before we could fully turn around, the opening was closed and Beatrix was gone.

Dawsyn wrapped her arms around herself and leaned into me. "She's getting old."

"I think she's been old for a while now," I tried to joke as I guided her toward the entry to Drago.

She grimaced. "But it never showed like it did just now."

"She'll be okay," I said as I pressed my palm into the rock, then cursed as the shimmer of the opening began to appear. "You can't get back in."

Dawsyn cocked her head. "What?"

"You no longer have a dragon tie to Drago," I explained. "I'm going to need to leave you here and then come back after I find Penn, so that he can pull the restrictions again."

She glanced back at the truck. "I'll just wait in there, but hurry. I doubt they have much time to prepare for an attack."

I was going to rush for more reasons than that. Leaving Dawsyn behind made my stomach churn, then fill with boulders, but we didn't have another choice.

I kissed her quickly, then walked through the portal into Drago, glancing back in time to see her wave just as I was sucked through to the other side.

Sticky heat covered my skin, and my shoulders shook with fury at the fucked-up situation we were in. Not only with Knox, but not having our bond reappear. As much as I considered wallowing in hatred for a moment, I knew time wasn't on our side.

I shifted to my dragon form and took to the skies, keeping low to not attract attention. I didn't spot any of the others that should have been out on patrol, which worried me further.

There were no signs of battle, but that didn't mean lives hadn't been lost in the nearly twelve hours we'd been gone.

With speed and efficiency, I was at the caves and shifting back to two feet in record time. I ran into the cave entrance and found Winter first. "Where is Penn?" I demanded.

She shrunk back against the dirt wall and pointed to the right. "In the dining hall. I just left there, and he was eating still."

I didn't bother with thanks. Instead, I continued my sprint, rounding corners as quickly as my legs would take me until I entered the area where a grouping of tables was set up.

My finger pointed at Penn, and he looked up at me with wide eyes. I suspected I looked almost feral after everything that had been happening as of late, the worst being that the warnings people had given Dawsyn and I about our bond weren't unwarranted.

"I need you now," I said gruffly.

He left his bowl of food behind and was out of his seat before I finished the sentence. "What's wrong?"

"I need you to reopen the portal to allow anyone in," I said in hushed tones. I wanted to believe we could trust everyone here, but there was no way to be certain.

He grimaced. "It already is. I went to check on things once it was safe again, and what was undone couldn't be redone without more time."

"Why the fuck didn't anyone tell me that?" I snapped, fisting my hands at my sides. "Never mind. I need to go."

I'd never even needed to leave Dawsyn behind. If something happened to her again...

Fuck!

My mood without her by my side was quickly souring, and I needed to get the fuck out of the caves before I tore someone's head off. Literally.

"Where is Fane?" I asked next.

"On patrol somewhere near the dark forest," he answered. "Everyone is preparing for an attack."

Well, at least one thing was going our way.

I turned abruptly and raced for the cave exit. I needed to shift and tell Fane what I knew as I rushed to get my mate back in my arms.

Otherwise, I was going to head right for the dark forest and burn the whole fucking place to bedrock. As soon as the snake living in the tunnel showed his damned face, I would remove it from his body.

Chapter Twenty-Five

DAWSYN

I was waiting in the truck and couldn't make my knee stop bouncing. Having the link to Knox gone was worth every bit of pain, but his threat wouldn't leave my mind. Neither would the concern that my bond with Cillian had yet to begin thrumming inside my chest again.

It also didn't help that I had no idea what he was walking into once he entered Drago again.

Had Knox already begun to cause mayhem? Was there even anyone left to help us?

All questions I wasn't going to get an answer to until my mate returned, and I badly needed a distraction. I started poking around Cillian's truck. Opening the glove box and then center console, the only thing I found was his phone in the cupholder.

As my fingers drummed over my thighs, I remembered River. Gods, I was such a shitty best friend.

I grabbed Cillian's phone and breathed out a sigh of relief when there was no passcode to get into it.

Thankfully, I had River's phone number memorized. The line rang once, and the grumbling voice of my best friend echoed through the line. "Where is she, Cillian?"

"She's right here," I said. "She's also really sorry she couldn't call sooner, and she loves you."

"Fuck, Dawsyn." River's harsh breath broke my heart. "I thought you were…"

"I know. I'm sorry. I couldn't let them kill you."

He growled. "You should have. You had no way to know you'd survive."

I wanted to tell him that a part of me hadn't, but he didn't need that kind of guilt by knowing I'd lost my fated bond. For now, at least. I'd fight to get that back once Knox was dealt with.

"I had a better shot than you," I replied. "And I'm safe now."

"Where are you?" he demanded.

"Getting ready to go back to Drago."

"Back? What do you mean *back*?" His panic made me smile. Not because he was suffering, but because of how much I knew he loved me.

I gave him a quick run-down of the last twenty-four hours. From my swift escape to my second near-death experience, then going to my pack before ending on a brief mention of our time with Beatrix.

"Fucking hell, D." He sighed heavily. "Come get me. I want to be there with you. You shouldn't be fighting this battle without your family."

A fissure opened in my chest. Thin, but deep as fuck.

He was right, but I loved them all too much to get them involved. Not unless we had no other choice.

"We don't even know if there's going to be a fight," I said.

"Bullshit," he spat. "Tell me where you are."

"I can't do that, Riv. I'm sorry. I know you're angry and scared right now—"

"You're fucking right I'm angry," he cut in. "My best friend was kidnapped by a psychotic dragon shifter and taken to another world, all because I let that damn warlock get the upper hand. You have no fucking clue how that feels. I'm supposed to be a protector, Dawsyn. Me. And I failed you. My best friend."

The crack in my chest got wider, and there was an ache inside me that only continued to grow as River spoke.

I wanted to cave. I wanted to ask Beatrix to bring him to me. I wanted him here just so I could wrap my arms around him and make him feel how much I didn't blame him for any of this shit.

"River..."

"Don't," he murmured. "Don't tell me this isn't my fault and that there's nothing I can do. I can't handle that right now."

"I'm sorry. I really am. Just let me get through today and I will come for you."

Even though I understood where his guilt and rage were coming from, I was still too selfish to put him in harm's way.

"This isn't fucking fair," he said, and I pictured him running a hand through his auburn hair and yanking on the ends with frustration.

"I know."

There was a stretch of silence between us, and I glanced

up to find Cillian standing in front of his truck. There was a softening in his eyes that told me he'd heard enough of our conversation to know how I was hurting.

"I love you, Dawsyn," River said softly. "We don't say that enough, and even though I hate that you put yourself in danger to save me, thank you."

"I love you, too. And I'd do it all over again if it meant keeping you alive. I won't live in a world without my best friend."

He grunted. "Just another realm."

"We are a long way from sorting that out, and if Drago is where we need to be, I'll only stay if you can visit anytime that you're not busy hunting down the bad guys and keeping the rest of the world safe."

"I want to be there with you now."

I knew he did, but I wasn't going to change my mind, so I just ignored his statement. "I need to go, but I'll call you tomorrow and figure out a way to come see you. I promise."

"You're entering a realm with a bloodthirsty dragon, hellbent on causing you and your mate suffering," River pointed out. "Don't make promises you're not sure you can keep, D."

"I'm going to be fine," I said. "There is a horde of dragons here that will make sure of that."

"Okay." The single word was said with heavy disbelief. "I love you."

"Love you, Riv. Always have, always will. But I need to go."

His response was tense silence.

"I'll see you tomorrow, okay?" I added.

"You better."

"I promise. Be prepared for all the tackle hugs. Just like when we were little."

He finally grunted out a laugh. "I'll hold you to it."

Our call ended, and I looked up again to find Cillian still standing in front of the truck. His hands were shoved in his pockets and his lips were pressed thin.

I got out of the cab, leaving his phone behind since it wouldn't do us any good in Drago, and headed straight to him, wrapping my hands around his neck and looking up at him. "What's wrong?"

"Nothing."

"Don't lie to me," I said firmly.

His eyes closed briefly before he stared closely at my face. "You have a lot of people who love you in your life."

"So do you."

His head shook. "I thought I did."

"Just because your grandmother turned on you doesn't mean the rest of your family has," I said. "What about your uncles? I know I haven't met them yet, but I'm sure that doesn't change anything."

The grimace on his face had my chest tightening. "There was so much going on before that I didn't tell you."

"Tell me what?"

"Someone murdered them in their home and left their bodies, likely for me to find." His words were barely above a whisper. "I'd shoved down my grief to find you, but seeing how close you and your family are... I'll never have that again."

Fuck. I hated this so much for him. I wanted to tell him that everything would be okay, but it was already so far from okay that I couldn't force the words to leave my mouth.

Instead, I moved my hands to his chest and held his stare. "I'll be your family, and that makes my family yours as well. They're a little insane at times, as you've already seen, but they'll always have your back."

A single tear fell down his right cheek. "Thank you."

"We'll give your uncles the proper goodbye they deserve as soon as we rip Knox's cold heart from his chest."

That had the side of his mouth turning up. "There's no *we* involved in that scenario. Knox is mine to kill."

As much as I wanted that bastard's blood, I knew Cillian was right. This was his fight, not mine. No matter how entangled I was in everything.

"Is the portal safe for me to go through?" I asked, knowing that we needed this moment together but also needed to hurry.

He nodded. "It's been open this whole time. Hopefully Knox hasn't figured that out."

Hell, I hoped not.

Cillian grabbed my hand from his chest and squeezed before leading us back toward the portal. "Ready?"

I nodded once and his grip tightened on me just like before. We stepped forward and then were quickly sucked through.

My eyes began to burn instantly, and I sucked in a breath. The air was thick with a dry heat and something else. I didn't know what, but whatever it was made every inhale feel like pins and needles were filling my lungs.

"What is that?" I asked, rubbing over my chest.

His brow creased. "What?"

"The air. It's tainted with something."

Cillian's chest expanded, and his frown deepened. "I don't sense anything."

Wolf?

It's wolfsbane, she replied. *Try not to breathe it in. You won't die, but too much will weaken us and potentially prevent us from shifting.*

Why the fuck didn't I know about this?

Because it's not supposed to exist any longer, she answered. *The last I knew, the plant had been eradicated.*

Clearly, not from Drago.

"The air is tainted with wolfsbane," I explained to Cillian. "I don't know if it affects dragons the same, but it will weaken me if I'm exposed to it for too long."

He snarled, then stepped away. "I'll shift and you can jump on. We'll be at the cave in no time."

I nodded, hoping the air hadn't been tainted that far out.

Cillian's dragon appeared in all his earthy colored goodness. Though, it was the splashes of blue that were my favorite. I jumped to his wing, then climbed onto his back, not nearly as unsure about riding up here as I'd been that first time.

He pushed from the ground and was racing through the sky within seconds.

I leaned forward, resting my body against his back while my heels dug into his sides and my hands gripped the bumps on his spine. My cheek pressed against his smooth scales, and I closed my eyes, soaking up his presence.

I searched deep inside myself, hoping for any sign of our bond, but still, there was nothing resembling the tether we'd had before. Nothing connecting us.

My heart cracked a little more, but before I could lose myself to grieving our bond, Cillian landed near the cave entrance.

Before he'd come to a full stop, I was jumping off him and taking a deep inhale. There was a slight sour taste to the air, but nothing like how it had been back near the portal we'd come through.

Just as Cillian shifted back to his human form, Lykem came sauntering out of the cave. His cheeks were still pale, but the spark was back in his eyes.

"About damn time the two of you got back," he joked. "We were going to start the party without you."

"What party?" I asked.

Lykem glanced at Cillian, then me. "We're ready to leave when you two are. The group came together this morning and decided there's no point in waiting to see what that fucker decides to do next. We're attacking today."

That was good, because I was already going to suggest that after what I'd heard. "He wants everyone dead. I broke the bond to him."

Lykem whistled. "Good to know."

"You're not fighting," Cillian said gruffly to his friend.

The dragon tossed his head back and laughed. "I'm a grown-ass man. You can't keep me out of this."

Cillian stood straighter and narrowed his eyes, heat rolling off him. "That's what you think now."

Lykem sobered and stepped closer. "I get that this is

more personal for you, but that fucker nearly killed me. You're not going to ask me to stand down."

Hell. He was just like River. Though, I had the added benefit of my best friend not knowing he could enter Drago just yet.

They had a brief stare-down, then Cillian's chest rumbled. "Fine, but if you die, that's on you. Not me."

The smirk that appeared on Lykem's face wasn't helping the situation. "We all know you'll still take it personal, but that's all part of the reason that I consider you my best friend, even if you like to think you don't have any real friends most of the time."

My hand wrapped around Cillian's forearm. "Come on. Let's go get ready."

I didn't need Lykem getting my mate more worked up than he already was. I needed Cillian to have as clear of a head as possible before going into this fight.

I'd only been through the cave and to Cillian's corner a couple times, but somehow, I managed to get us back without getting lost.

He wasn't any calmer by the time we got there, and I did the only thing I could think of to clear his mind.

I shoved him against the wall with one hand, wrapped the other around his neck, and brought his mouth to mine. A growl rumbled from deep inside me, one full of equal parts frustration and need.

Frustration because everything about being with Cillian was complicated and messy, but none of that mattered in the end, because I needed him.

Bond or not, he was who I wanted, and I was going to make sure he understood that.

His fingers tangled in my hair, and he angled my head to the side, deepening the kiss. Before I knew what was happening, he reversed our positions and had me pinned against the rock wall of the cave.

It was dark in our little corner, but I didn't need the light to see the spark returning to his eyes or to know the rapid rise and fall of his chest was exactly what I'd hoped for.

He pressed his forehead against mine, breaking the kiss. "You're everything I never expected."

The words whispered over my cheek, and I grinned. "And I always will be. Predictability isn't really my thing."

That finally had his lips tugging upward, then the smile fell just as quickly. "The bond didn't come back."

I held my palm over his heart and looked deeply into his eyes. "I don't need a bond to know what I feel in here." Then, I covered my own heart. "And in here. We can still have a chosen mate bond. We can still choose each other, and there won't be anyone that can stop us in the end."

"You deserve better," he muttered.

My fingers fisted his shirt. "I deserve whatever the hell I want, and I want you, Cillian." I slid a hand between us, down his rippling muscles, over his jeans, then cupped his hard cock. "And you want me, too."

"That I fucking do." His words were feral, and the air around us heated. Something in him seemed to snap inside, and I was absolutely here for it.

With one hand still tangled in my hair, he trailed his fingers down the side of my neck, along my shoulder, then down my ribs, letting his thumb graze the side of my breasts as he went.

I sucked in a breath, having no idea what his intentions were. He'd been the definition of proper since finding my way back to him, and while I appreciated how much he respected me, if he wanted to fuck me against this wall, I was also perfectly okay with that.

He moved closer and growled in my ear. "Your scent is driving me fucking insane." His lips pressed against my neck just before his teeth scraped over the sensitive skin. "But you deser—"

"If you say I deserve better one more time, you're going to have the worst blue balls in the history of mankind," I threatened with a rumble in my chest.

I grabbed onto his face and kissed him again with all the pent-up need I'd been suppressing because he'd been right. There hadn't been a right time or place for us to have this moment together, but I was tired of waiting.

I needed him. His touch, his passion, his body.

And he needed me, too, even if he wouldn't admit it out loud.

"Touch me, Cillian," I said softly against his lips, and as if all the stars had finally aligned, he put me out of my damn misery.

He unbuttoned my jeans and slid his hand further down, beneath my underwear and over my clit before slipping between my wet folds.

I inhaled deeply, my chest expanding and fingers digging into his shoulders as my head lolled back.

Fucking hell.

He pushed a finger inside me, making my inner muscles instantly contract. His hand moved in and out, while my hips matched the movements.

With his other hand, he gripped my chin to bring my head back and pressed his lips to mine. Our tongues quickly became tangled while his hand fucked me into the next century.

His mouth captured my moans, and I clung to him like he was my lifeline. In that moment, it felt as if that was the truest thought in existence. My body needed his and the release I only wanted from him.

When he slipped another finger inside me and his palm created beautiful friction over my clit, I nearly died from the relief.

Desire unfurled from my core, spreading down my legs and up my chest at the same time. I deepened our kiss so that I didn't scream within the echoing walls of the cave tunnels and held on for the ride.

My body rocked against his, taking everything that it needed as I clung to him. My pussy tightened around his hand and then...euphoria.

I crumpled against Cillian's body, and he held me against his chest softly, kissing the side of my face when I could no longer hold my head up.

"I mean, I knew I needed that, but I didn't know how *much* I needed that," I said breathily, trying to regain my composure so I could at least hold myself up.

He brushed my hair back and he smiled down at me. "I needed it, too."

The back of my hand grazed over his erection. "You need a lot more than that."

"As much as I want to agree," he said softly, "we're out of time. But you helped get my head clear, which was also needed. I know what has to be done and not much else matters until then."

"And what's that?"

"Killing Knox so that he can't ever hurt you again."

That was a plan I was perfectly okay with.

Chapter Twenty-Six

CILLIAN

The fury I'd been consumed with as soon as I'd left Dawsyn's side to make sure she'd be able to get through the portal had slowly dissipated. Though, when I'd heard her conversation with River, that rage had been mixed with something more complicated. My mate was giving up a lot to be with me, and I wouldn't take that for granted.

When she'd pushed me against that wall, I'd known there was no denying her needs, just like I'd been unable to before at the river. I'd smelled her arousal, and there wasn't a single part of me that could find the want to disappoint her, privacy be damned.

Though, declining my own needs wasn't a problem. I was still adamant that the first time we had sex, we wouldn't be rushed or somewhere that we couldn't fully enjoy ourselves. Letting her do anything to me was going to lead to more. There'd be no stopping the drive to claim her once we took things further. I knew that without a single doubt in my mind.

That didn't mean my choice was easy to stick with. I did my best to focus on the fact that once this fight was over...she'd be all mine.

Once we righted ourselves, Dawsyn and I headed back to the front of the cave where a group of others were already gathered outside the entrance.

Lykem, Clay, Fane, and a few others spoke quietly until we approached, then made room for us to join them.

"Are you ready?" Lykem asked.

I nodded, but I wasn't sure they were. "Do you have a plan, or are we just going to show up and hope for the best?"

He gestured toward Dawsyn. "Since she said we won't be able to get in on our own, I figured our best plan of attack was just to attack."

My friend wasn't wrong, but he also wasn't right.

"If they feel safe within their underground bunker, they're not going to come out when we have the advantage," I said. "And we need to get in more than we need them to come out. Knox might have the door sealed to only open for him, but that doesn't mean the tree is the only way to get inside."

Dawsyn grinned at me. "Are we going to blow up the ground?"

She seemed a little too pleased with that for someone who I felt pretty confident hadn't murdered anyone before.

"Not exactly," I replied. "I think if we bring in rocks big enough to weaken the surface above the tunnels, then we can open up several spots with our claws that will allow those who are fighting underground to get in. We don't want to kill anyone with an explosion who doesn't deserve to die."

Like my father, I thought, but didn't say.

I had no clue how he'd ended up as Knox's prisoner, and I wasn't sure how the others would feel about wanting to get him out of there, but my father hadn't been far from my mind since Dawsyn had told me he was there.

Clay glanced at Dawsyn. "How many other prisoners were there?"

"Only one that I saw, but that doesn't mean much," she answered. "The rooms people are kept in are soundproof with no light. There could have been a dozen souls down there." She then looked up at me. "I'd like to be the one to go down there and free them. I know where they're at and can run as my wolf within the underground hallways."

I wanted to tell her no. I didn't want her out of my sight, but more than that, I also knew I didn't want her anywhere near Knox again.

"Lykem will go with you," I said, knowing that he was better off not fighting in his dragon form after the injuries he'd just sustained. "Nobody should be working alone today. Pick someone to fight alongside and stick with them. We have no idea who these dragons are or what they might be capable of. If they won't stand down, strike them down. We can't hesitate."

Heads nodded all around, and Dawsyn was still grinning before she began to speak again. "Do you have weapons? Not everyone will come out of the bunker, so more of you will need to prepare to be fighting in your human forms."

Clay patted his side, where I assumed a knife or two

were hidden by his shirt. "We already have that covered. There are more blades in the storage room that we gathered yesterday for people to use."

"How many total do we have coming with us?" I asked.

"Twenty-seven," Lykem answered.

That wasn't as many as I'd thought there would be, but hopefully it was enough.

I glanced up at the sky. It was darker than usual, and the air was growing heavier, which reminded me that Dawsyn didn't need to be outside any longer than necessary with the wolfbane particles somehow floating around.

"We leave in ten," I said, then grabbed my mate's hand and led her back inside where the air was cleaner and we could find weapons.

She smiled at me again as we walked, so I asked, "Why are you looking at me like that?"

"Because you're a leader here and don't even know it," she answered. "Those dragons respect you and would follow you into any battle."

"We respect each other and would do the same for any of us."

She shrugged. "Maybe, but they listened to you. Trusted you when you came up with the plan and seemed to agree to it without question. Drago may not have conventional leaders like we do back home, but you're one of them, whether you admit it or not."

I wanted to disagree with her. Uncle Jerome had been a leader. Even my grandmother had been before she'd turned on us. But that was never me.

Though, I couldn't deny there had been a drive to take

charge and protect the dragons here bleeding through me for weeks now.

I was only doing what was best. That didn't make me a leader.

We arrived at the storage area where there were three tables set out and only a few blades still left on each. Dawsyn reached for a group of smaller ones and began tucking them into the sides of her socks then in her back pockets.

"Don't you want something bigger?" I asked.

"Bigger isn't always better." She winked. "Thanks to my gender and size, I'll be underestimated by most everyone we encounter, but I'm fast. I can move quicker with a smaller weapon."

She made a point that had me changing my selection. I grabbed two smaller blades that were tucked into my boots and one larger one in a sheath that I could clip to my pants.

Dawsyn turned to leave the tunnel, but I grabbed her hand and pulled her back to me. "I know I can't tell you what to do, but that doesn't mean I can't ask more from you than I should. If it comes to your life or someone else's, choose yours. That includes my father. I've lived without everyone else. I don't want to know what it feels like to live without you."

She pushed up onto her toes and kissed me. "I'm an alpha, and I'm the daughter of a Luna Marked wolf. You may not completely understand what that means, but just know you don't need to worry about me. I'll be okay."

"How do you know when you've never fought dragons before?" I asked, appreciating her confidence, but still unable to stop feeling the need to protect her.

She pressed a palm to her chest. "In here. I have my wolf in my head as well. She's been off in her quiet place for the last few days, channeling the new energy we felt before, figuring out how we can best use it to our advantage. I may not have experience battling dragons, but they haven't fought me either." She paused, then added, "I escaped that bunker once. I'll do it again."

My hand wrapped around her neck, and I kissed her hard. "Just be safe."

"I will. I promise."

"I'm going to have to shift and fly while you stay on the ground, but I'll stay as close to you as possible."

She squeezed my hand and offered me a sweet smile. "Don't worry about me."

The words fell on deaf ears.

"Let's go." I led us back outside, seeing no point in furthering the conversation and letting my mind get wound up again. Nothing was going to change. Dawsyn was right. She was an alpha and, while I didn't grow up around them, I understood the meaning. She would do whatever she thought was best, and there wasn't a damn thing anyone could say to change her mind.

When we arrived back outside, lightning was streaking across the sky and landing closer to the caves than ever before.

Clay and Lykem were directing people who weren't fighting to start traveling north, as far from here as possible.

"And when do we come back?" Sereph asked, with Daron by her side.

I suddenly understood why we had less fighters than I'd hoped. Some of them had to stay with the others.

"When we come for you or never at all," Clay answered her grimly.

That had her face paling and throat bobbing, but it was the truth. While we had the team to win, Knox was ready for us and there were no guarantees in this battle.

"We're ready to go," Lykem said once Sereph and Daron had left to start the evacuation of the cave.

"So are we." My hold on Dawsyn tightened as the lie left my mouth. I'd never be ready to head into a fight with my mate.

But I also knew when I was out of options. None of this could be avoided.

Our group of nearly thirty dragon shifters walked away from the cave, some with their other halves still clinging to them, others alone and prepared to die if that was what this came to.

The air was thick and the mood tense, but we were in this together and that was most important.

As soon as we were out of the tree line, I turned to Dawsyn, wrapping my arms around her again and pressing my mouth to her ear. "When we're done here, I'm going to take you somewhere far away from anyone else."

"I will gladly let you."

Her steady heartbeat thrummed against me, calming my nerves as I anchored myself to her, even without the tether of our bond. I closed my eyes and just focused on my mate, knowing that no matter what, she was mine.

Now and always.

Chapter Twenty-Seven

DAWSYN

The further we moved away from the caves, the harder it was for me to breathe. Though, not impossible. I wasn't sure how Knox had gotten a hold of wolfsbane and had filtered it through the air like this, but I was going to find whatever remnants of the plant are in Drago and burn them to ash.

As promised, Cillian stayed close to me, flying above as I raced over the ground as my wolf. Even though the air burned our lungs, my wolf was charged with energy.

The meditating did you good, I said.

We're not Luna Marked, she replied, even though that wasn't where I was going to take the conversation just before a fight.

But we're not a normal wolf shifter, either, I countered.

No, and this wasn't a gift from the moon goddess, she said.

That had my pulse increasing. *Then, where the hell did the boost of power come from?*

The only thing I've been able to tell is the bond with Cillian.

Yet, the bond with him is gone and we're still glowing...

I wanted to believe her, to grasp on to the hope that just because the physical presence of our bond hadn't returned didn't mean it was never coming back. Yet, the fear of it not being true made me believe otherwise.

It was too late for further conversation.

Lightning and fire began zipping through the sky toward us, some sailing past and toward the caves.

I sent up a silent prayer that the others had already left and nobody would be hurt, then returned my focus to right in front of me.

Bolts of dark energy hit the ground, sending tremors through the earth and creating cracks.

We sidestepped and increased our speed while also watching the sky to make sure Cillian was okay.

He was carrying a massive boulder within his clawed feet, and his wings flapped steadily. White energy crackled around his scales and when the next stream of fire came for us, my mate counteracted it with his own powers.

The white magic around him funneled toward the front of his body, then sent a bolt of lightning toward the flames.

I watched in amazement how the two energies collided, wrapping around each other, fighting for dominance, then exploding with a loud bang. Rain in the form of orange and white specks fell over us, but no longer held enough power to harm anyone.

We were entering the dark forest then, and a chill raced

down my spine. The last time I'd been in here, I'd lost my shit. I couldn't let that happen again.

We won't, my wolf promised.

My job was to lead the dragons toward the tree, then howl loudly as soon as I got there so they could start dropping the rocks to weaken the ground enough for us to break through from the top instead of trying to get past the door that supposedly only Knox could open.

Running toward where I'd been held captive felt wrong, but there wasn't anything that would stop me from going back. There was at least one person who needed saving, and I'd made myself a promise that I'd come back for him, even before I knew he was Cillian's father.

It might have taken us some time to get back here, but now that we were, I wasn't leaving until the job was done.

The forest was darker than I remembered, and the air burned not only my lungs now, but my skin as well. Though, in my wolf form, I could see further than when Knox had forced me along.

How the hell is the wolfsbane penetrating the air so thoroughly? I asked, not really expecting an answer, which was good because a dragon came out of nowhere, wings tucked in at its sides and horned head pointed directly at us.

My wolf rolled us over the ground, pushing our body as close to the surface as possible. When the dragon flew at us with his claws out, he only managed to nick a front leg.

In return, we ripped open the underside of his tail before getting back to our feet and running faster toward the tree so we could alert the other dragons.

The attacking dragon had turned around, but not

quickly, thanks to its bigger size and all the trees, which allowed me to get ahead.

With renewed determination, I felt the energy inside us rising and our speed increasing. The dragon didn't seem to be able to do that in such tight quarters.

We were far enough ahead now that I wasn't as concerned with the beast behind us as I was with what we might find once we got to the tree where the door was.

At the last second, I cut left and decided the door wasn't where the dragons were going to be aiming anyway with their boulders. I needed to put them closer to the underground tunnel.

The flapping of wings came closer, and the trees were opening up more in this area, but that didn't stop the howl from ripping from my chest.

Dozens of dragons roared in response, and then I was racing back in the other direction to avoid being crushed.

Boulders dropped from high up in the sky, and I caught sight of Cillian again. His claws were empty this time, and the ground beneath my paws shook as more dragons did their jobs.

I then realized that there was nowhere for Cillian, or really any of the others, to land and shift back.

Apparently, they weren't the least bit concerned.

I watched in amazement as Cillian flew closer to the tree line and then his body shimmered, growing smaller in size before he transformed back to his human form about fifteen feet from the ground.

Awesome fucking trick, I thought before shifting as well and running toward him.

He wrapped me in his arms. "You're hurt. I smelled blood."

"There was a dragon back there, but I lost him at some point." I glanced behind him. "Is it working?"

"Not as well as we'd hoped, but we'll get in or they'll come out. Either way, this is happening."

That was good, because I had so much adrenaline pumping through my veins, I wasn't sure I could *not* fight someone at this point.

A crease formed between his eyes. "You're still glowing even as you are now." His hands moved over my arms. "It's faint, but there's definitely something there."

I glanced down and, sure enough, there was a soft silver glow above my skin.

The energy is protecting us from the wolfsbane, my wolf said. *We should be unconscious by now.*

Well, shit. That was rather helpful, and I relayed that same information to Cillian.

"I don't understand your shifter abilities, but I'm damn sure grateful for them."

Him and me both.

Another roar sounded in the sky and even more from further north.

Cillian's hold on my arms tightened. "They dropped the last boulder. It's time. Stick to the plan, Dawsyn. Find my dad if you can, but more importantly, get the hell out of there before things escalate."

I nodded. I had every intention of doing just that, but it didn't mean I would find the quickest escape, depending on the condition Darius was in.

"And you're going back up there?" I asked him. He hadn't seemed sure what his form of attack would be.

"For the moment. I want to see if Knox comes out first before going in," he replied. "I won't miss my chance to end him."

The sky cracked with more lightning, causing both of us to look up.

"I need to go," Cillian said, an uneasiness lacing his words.

"I'll be fine," I reminded him with a smile, trying to lighten the mood. "My freaky wolf powers will make sure of that."

"They better," he grumbled, then wrapped his arms around me one more time, kissing me so thoroughly that my toes began to curl inside my boots just as he pulled away. "I'm going to go before I change my mind."

I gave him a light shove. "I'll see you soon."

"But not soon enough," he added as he jogged far enough away to begin shifting. His dragon body was much too big to be in the forest, but that didn't seem to stop him.

With what seemed like little effort, Cillian's head pushed trees out of the way, causing them to fall to the earth, then he spread his wings before taking flight.

"Show-off," I muttered before transforming back to my wolf.

It was time to sneak back inside the place I'd fought so hard to escape.

We ran back toward where the boulders were dropped. Dragons were dipping low to the ground and clawing at the dirt in rapid succession until they broke the top completely. The openings weren't big enough for any of them to fit, and neither were the tunnels, but I wasn't waiting for a dragon to lead the way.

My wolf spotted the nearest hole. We were going in.

At least, that was the plan until Lykem dropped from the sky right in our path. He crossed his arms over his chest and tsked. "Did you forget you were supposed to stick with me?"

Not exactly, I thought. I'd just hoped I could get away with going by myself. I didn't need a babysitter.

But a little back-up never killed anyone.

I wanted to disagree, but my wolf wasn't wrong.

We yipped at Lykem, then nodded toward the hole.

He glanced back and shook his arms out. "Let's have some fun, Wolf Girl."

Oh, I intended to.

He jumped through first, and just as I followed him, a fist came flying for my wolf's head.

Before it could connect, Lykem had the guy by the throat and slammed him into the hard rock wall with a smirk on his face. "Look at me coming in handy already."

He was a little too proud of that fact as he tied a rope around the guy's hands behind his back. "No killing unless we have to."

That was a part of the plan I was more than okay with. I'd been trained to kill, but I'd yet to actually do so. Though, I knew I could without blinking an eye if it meant saving an innocent life.

Once he was done, I glanced in both directions, trying to correlate where we'd jumped in with where the door in the tree was.

We were further down than I'd been. Though, I felt

rather confident that we needed to head right, then turn left somewhere up ahead.

I led the way with Lykem right behind me, him running and managing to keep up with my wolf.

Three men charged toward us, and I glanced at Lykem. He'd just been badly injured the day before, yet I couldn't see any signs that he'd already tired or was too weak to fight. I just had to trust that he was as strong on the inside as he was appearing on the outside.

"I'll get baldy on the right," he said. "You get the left and we'll hope the third doesn't blindside one of us."

That was as good of a plan as we were going to come up with. Given the tight quarters, there wasn't going to be a chance of separating the group to lessen their advantage.

We met the three men head on. Lykem was swinging punches with one hand and swiping out with a knife in the other.

My wolf had her teeth bared and claws at the ready. We attacked the guy on the left as planned, attempting to only knock him out, given how easily Lykem had done that to the first attacker. Except this one wasn't as easily taken down.

He had a glowing blade in his hand and winked just before he swiped at me. We dodged out of the way, but he was quick with another attempt. This time the knife sliced cleanly through my wolf's front leg, preventing us from putting any pressure on it.

Sorry, wolf, I said. *I don't think bringing a wolf to a knife fight is going to be helpful this time.*

She snarled and backed up, then allowed me to shift back without any resistance.

As soon as I was on two feet, I checked my arm where she'd been cut. It wasn't deep, but blood still trickled down my arm.

I surged forward with two blades in hand from my back pockets. Just before I moved to cut my attacker in return, I dropped down and slid toward him.

His knife barely missed the top of my head, and mine cut through his inner thighs.

The roar he bellowed had me grinning, but not for long.

I caught the third attacker jumping onto Lykem's back while he was still fighting the bald one.

Deciding mine was incapacitated enough, I jumped into Lykem's fight without thinking.

As soon as I grabbed on to the third man, a shot of electricity went through me and my body was forced back, slamming into the wall.

I had to blink several times before I could get back up. "Fuck, that hurt," I muttered.

Though, I had to figure something else out and soon, because Lykem was worse off than I realized.

His entire body shook, and he was seconds from having his neck sliced up.

That could have been you if you'd gone ahead without him, my wolf reminded me, then added something actually helpful. Use your knife to dig a chunk of rock from the wall, then smash it over the guy's head.

That I could do.

Then I had a better idea once I began to turn around.

The man I'd already taken out was bent over, hugging his legs. Instead of wasting time we didn't have getting a rock, I grabbed the guy and lifted him up just enough to throw him at the others.

He was heavy, but between the adrenaline and new energy inside me, I had no problem with the action.

As soon as his body hit the one with the electricity power, all four of them tumbled to the ground. I had no idea if I'd interrupted the energy enough to make things safe for me, but I had to help Lykem.

I charged forward again, knife in hand and without thinking about the potential consequences, I drove the blade into the neck of the third attacker.

My muscles tensed as I waited for the pain, but it never came, and Lykem was able to get out from underneath them, only one bad cut on his collarbone.

"Thanks," he huffed before reaching down to the bald one. Lykem picked him up, then slammed him against the wall twice.

This time, there was no point in tying the attacker up. This one wasn't waking up.

The one I'd been fighting held his hands up. "I won't fight back."

Lykem kicked him in the ribs. "Then, you can live, but that doesn't mean it won't hurt."

He tied him up, and I glanced at the one I'd stabbed in the neck. Yeah, he wasn't waking up either.

I'd thought I'd feel more at having been responsible for taking a life, but knowing Lykem was alive because of my choice made any guilt I might have felt otherwise become non-existent.

Once there were no more threats, Lykem nodded at me. "Where to now?"

"Straight ahead until we see the tunnels start to appear on the left," I said.

The pounding of footfalls sounded behind us, and I tensed, ready to fight again, but Lykem placed a hand on my shoulder. "They're friendly."

Two shifters I didn't recognize joined us. "Need us to do anything about these ones?"

Lykem shook his head. "Go ahead and make sure we don't run into any other problems."

Without questioning anything, they did just that and we followed a little slower behind them.

After another five minutes, we finally made it to the cell area. I shifted back to two feet as soon as I saw the door I'd been looking for. Only it was open and not sealed shut like it should have been.

"Fuck," I muttered, jerking on the handle.

There was a momentary relief when I saw someone still in the dark room, but that was dashed away just as quickly when I realized he was bleeding profusely from a head wound.

"Darius," I said, kneeling next to him. "I'm here to help you. I need you to wake up."

His body was beaten badly and wasn't moving, but he was at least breathing.

"That's Darius?" Lykem asked. "Are you sure?"

My head whipped back. "What the fuck do you mean am I sure? Don't you recognize him?"

If I'd been wrong and this wasn't Cillian's father... I wasn't sure how my mate would take that disappointment after all he'd been through lately.

Lykem lowered himself next to me and grabbed the

man by his shoulders, brushing long tangled hair away from his face. "I mean, he could be. It's been a couple decades since I saw him. He used to be larger than life. This man is..."

Not that, I thought.

"Even if he's not the Darius we thought he was, we still have to help him," I said. "Carry him in your arms and be fucking careful."

"Easy, Wolf Girl," he rumbled in return. "I'm not the one you need to be aggressive with. If I'm carrying him, you'll need to watch out for more attackers."

I was fully aware of that, but also glad Lykem had stopped me from doing this by myself. I'd have been fucked before I'd even gotten to the cells, and I wasn't too proud to admit that.

I just had to keep hoping that Cillian had been just as successful as we'd been.

If not, my wolf was about to spill a hell of a lot more blood.

Chapter Twenty-Eight

CILLIAN

Flying away from Dawsyn was hard, but as soon as I shifted, I'd made sure Lykem knew to find her given how certain I felt that she wouldn't wait for him before running headfirst into those tunnels.

As I took to the skies, I searched for Knox's dragon, but after ten minutes of looking and keeping an eye on things below, he was nowhere to be seen. Not only did him not coming out to fight like a man frustrate me, but so did the number of dragons working with Knox. I was more than a little disappointed in how many dragons had been hiding out here.

They started to crawl out of the ground, shifting almost immediately. Some of them I knew and most of them I didn't, but either way, I didn't understand how they could have decided to work to destroy their own world. Though, they weren't my problem at the moment. Knox was. I stayed out of the fight as much as I was able until I could find him.

The dragons that had come with us were holding their

own. None of the ones supporting Knox seemed to be able to do anything special, but that didn't mean we could let our guard down.

When it seemed like the numbers had shifted to our benefit, I flew to the ground and decided it was time for me to head inside the tunnel.

As I landed between already demolished trees, my dragon's head jerked to the right. There were no sounds coming from that way, but there was heavy energy pulsing from the trees that I hadn't sensed when we'd been higher in the sky.

I shifted back to my human form, because getting through the dense forest as my dragon would only hinder me. Then I ran.

There was no way to know if I was making the right choice moving away from the fight and the tunnels, but I couldn't ignore the pull toward the power I'd sensed.

It was heavy and most of all familiar. Not because I'd encountered it before, but because it tasted like family.

All blood-related dragons shared a certain scent. My family smelled of the air after a fierce storm. Fresh yet so crisp, it was almost like pins and needles on your skin.

And it was a scent that came directly from my mother's more powerful family line. Another reason why my gut told me that it was Knox I was suddenly chasing after.

With my uncle dead, there shouldn't have been anyone else with that scent other than me, and if Knox had it and I hadn't realized it before because I'd been so concerned with keeping Dawsyn safe, then that meant he was my mother's child.

Even though I'd had the same thought before, the longer I considered the possibility, the less it made sense.

I could have understood if my dad had fathered a child and didn't know about it before he met my mother, but there was no scenario in which my mother could have had a baby and didn't know, nor could I have imagined her abandoning a child.

Yet, that seemed to be exactly what happened to Knox. So, what the hell happened all those years ago?

That was a question that had the possibility of staying with me my whole life. I didn't suspect Knox was going to be forthcoming with information, and I wasn't going to allow him to live any longer than it took me to get my claws around his throat.

I came to an abrupt stop when I saw the glow of a tree. A man stepped forward that I shared no similarities with other than our scent.

A smirk grew on his sharp face, making the scar on his cheek stand out. "Cillian. I've been waiting for you."

"You never should have touched her," I snarled. My dragon's rage at seeing the man who stole our bond with Dawsyn had my own ire increasing by the second.

"I wanted your attention and now I have it, *Brother*." His stance was relaxed as he stepped closer, seeming not to care that I was about to rip his throat out.

My fingers curled into fists at my sides and my chest heaved. "I could have been your brother, but you chose differently."

His haunting laugh echoed around us. "*I* chose? Oh, how young and naïve you are, Cillian."

"You killed my uncles, stole my mate, and burned half

the city down while murdering thousands of dragons in the process." I turned my body, preparing to attack as he got within striking distance. "Unless you're about to tell me someone else is controlling you, *you* chose this path, and it ends here."

Whatever had happened to him, I no longer had the desire to know. The fact he'd touched my mate was already enough to end him. Everything else just proved my motivations weren't unfounded or selfish.

My right fist connected with his jaw, sending him tumbling back several steps, but I didn't stop there. I charged forward, hands out and claws extended past my fingertips.

Scales appeared over my skin, giving me an added layer of protection as I reached for Knox's neck.

He sidestepped me, regaining his footing quickly. "You're not strong enough to hurt me, dear brother. Why try?"

Oh, I could and I would. Severely.

I ignored his taunting and struck again, this time going for his legs. My claws cut through his thigh, hopefully straight through his femoral artery.

He barely even flinched, then he laughed as his leg buckled. "Is that all you have?"

My chest burned with fire, and I kneeled over him, pressing my knee into his chest as I bent forward to choke him.

Knox wasn't fighting back, though.

After all he'd done and destroyed, him giving up now made no sense. I wanted to stop and question what was happening—or more accurately, what *wasn't* happening—

but Knox twisted as if he was about to roll out from underneath me and I let my wrath get the best of me.

"No!" I roared in his face, tightening the grip around his neck.

His eyes darkened, showing the evil I'd already known he held inside. "Then, fucking kill me, Cillian. What are you waiting for? For Mommy to come back and tell us to be nice to each other?"

"Don't fucking speak of her." My heart hammered in my chest. I wanted so badly to end him like I'd come here to do, but something was stopping me. Knox wanted to die. He was begging for this, but why?

Why, after all he'd done?

"Maybe you're waiting for Dawsyn to come find us," he taunted. "I've been wondering if she regretted leaving me to go back to you."

A heaviness settled over me, not like a weight to bear, but one to be unleashed, and there was no stopping its power. The moment he'd mentioned Dawsyn, I had no control over my actions. I no longer gave a shit why he wanted to die. All I knew was that he needed to cease breathing.

My clawed fingers dug into his neck, breaking the skin while Knox grinned like a fucking maniac.

Though, he at least remained silent for the few beats it took for me to squeeze the life out of him.

His head lolled to the side, going unconscious first, then his heart slowed until it stuttered to a full stop.

Blood from where my claws had broken the skin coated my hands, and my body shook with unused adrenaline.

"Fuck!" I screamed.

Why hadn't he fought me, and what had I just done?

My gut twisted as if I was supposed to already know, yet I didn't feel sorry for taking his life. My mother might have birthed him, but Knox would never have been my family.

I stood up, thinking of Dawsyn next. The need to know she was okay consumed the rest of my thoughts. The consequences of killing my brother could wait until I had my mate back in my arms, safe and sound.

With one last glance at the ground, my eyes took in Knox's still-lifeless body, half expecting him to not actually be dead. Yet...his skin was already paling, his heart no longer beating, and no part of him even flinched.

He was well and truly dead.

Knowing that I wasn't going to figure out what still had my stomach churning by standing here, I started walking away, ignoring the uncomfortableness stirring inside me.

My feet began to run back toward the tunnels, toward my mate, and when I was halfway there, I could hear Dawsyn yelling my name from what seemed like too far away.

"I'm right here," I called back, my heart in my throat. She'd better be okay.

Her glowing form reached me quicker than I'd expected. There was blood splatter on her face and a few cuts and bruises on her arms that I could see, but nothing she wouldn't heal from. Though, her eyes were wide and full of concern as she struggled to breathe from the intensity of the run.

"You can't kill Knox," she said, grabbing my arms.

"Why?" I asked instead of telling her it was too late.

"Darius woke up as we were carrying him," she said.

"All he kept repeating was 'don't let my son kill him.' I don't know why, but he was frantic."

Lykem came running with my frail father in his arms.

I stepped forward, my eyes blinking rapidly as my brain tried to process that it was really him. My dad was alive. After all these years.

There was a second of relief before he looked up at me from where he lay draped in Lykem's arms. "Did you kill him, Son?"

I nodded just once, and his eyes fluttered closed. "It's too late then."

"Too late for what?" I asked firmly, but he didn't answer. His breathing evened out, and he was unconscious again.

"Too late to save Drago," a familiar voice sounded from behind me.

I turned to find my grandmother standing there, dressed in a loose, charcoal-colored dress that fell to her ankles.

"You have some fucking nerve showing up here, Estelle," I spat.

Her eyes rolled. "And you have no clue what you're talking about. I tried to warn you, but you didn't listen."

I stood taller and crossed my arms over my chest. "When the fuck did you try to warn me? Before or after you helped Knox steal my mate?"

My father groaned, causing my attention to turn back to him. "Don't speak to Nannio that way."

"You have no clue what she's done," I replied roughly as tension consumed my body.

He coughed, spitting up blood in the process. "Yes, I

do, and you need her, so whatever you're angry about, you need to get over it."

"Why? Knox is dead, and she should be next for helping him."

My father's pale body shook. "Your brother's heart might have stopped beating, but he isn't dead, Son."

Estelle stepped closer to our small group, but I made sure to keep distance between us as she spoke. "Darius is right. Knox needed to die by his own blood, and you've just helped him become exactly what he needed to be in order to truly destroy Drago. And he won't stop there. He intends to head for Earth next."

"What exactly is he?" Dawsyn asked as I stood there consumed with wrath.

My grandmother kept her gaze on me as she answered. "An Ember dragon."

Son of a bitch.

Thank you so much for reading A Dragon's Curse! Add A Dragon's Fate—the final book in this trilogy—to your wish list or preorder today! This will release June 29th, 2023.
Also, feel free to join my reader group Heather Renee's Book Warriors to get early sneak peeks of what's to come!

In the meantime, make sure you've read the other Mystics and Mayhem books so you can fully enjoy all of the character cameos as the series continues! Find more about those on the next few pages.

Mystics and Mayhem

If this is your first trip into the Mystics and Mayhem, welcome! Hello again, if not :) For our first timers, the series you're reading—The Hidden Realm—is technically the start of the second phase within Mystics and Mayhem and the fifth series within this world!

Want to catch up with the rest of the books while you wait (hopefully) patiently for the next book? Check out the list of all the Paranormal Romance stories included in this world below. Ones where you'll always find fierce, yet relatable leading ladies and strong alpha males who sweep them off their feet, along with humor and intrigue that will keep you turning the pages.

While you don't have to read the series in any particular order as there are no spoilers between each trilogy, this is the recommended reading order:

Broken Court (Lucinda and Finn)
Dark Fae Cursed — Dark Fae Freed — Dark Fae Unrivaled
Luna Marked (Cait and Roman—Dawsyn's Parents)

Wolf Kissed — Wolf Taken — Wolf Mated
Scorned by Blood (Amersyn and Maciah)
Vampire Heir — Vampire Ash — Vampire Vow
Fated to the Wolf (Andie and Foster)
Shifted Magic — Altered Magic — Forged Magic
The Hidden Realm (Dawsyn and Cillian)
A Dragon's Wolf — A Dragon's Curse — A Dragon's Fate

Hopefully there will be plenty more series to come as the years continue, but for now, if you want to stay up to date on all the bookish things, or have any questions, join my reader group Heather Renee's Book Warriors on Facebook or send me an email anytime at HeatherReneeAuthor@yahoo.com.

I hope you enjoy this world as much as I have!

Also by Heather Renee

MYSTICS AND MAYHEM SERIES

Fated to the Wolf

A complete New Adult Witch and Wolf series (dual POV) featuring an abandoned witch, a rogue wolf, and their broken bond.

Scorned by Blood

A complete New Adult Vampire series featuring a supernatural hunter and the sexy vampire bound to protect her no matter the cost.

Luna Marked

A complete New Adult wolf shifter series (dual POV) featuring a strong-willed leading lady and a patient, yet fierce alpha male.

Broken Court

A complete New Adult Urban Fantasy series featuring an unconventional and anti-heroine leading lady, a broody love interest, and a fae kingdom with a vile king.

INDIVIDUAL SERIES

Raven Point Pack Series

A complete Upper Young Adult Paranormal Romance series featuring wolves, witches, vengeance, and fated mates.

Shadow Veil Academy

A complete Upper Young Adult Urban Fantasy Academy series featuring shifters, elves, witches, and more.

Elite Supernatural Trackers

A complete New Adult Urban Fantasy series featuring witches, demons, a smart-mouthed female lead, alpha males, and a snarky fairy sidekick.

Royal Fae Guardians

A complete Young Adult Urban Fantasy series featuring fae, magic users, a sweet romance, along with snark and humor.

Blood of the Sea Series

A complete Young Adult Paranormal Romance series featuring vampires, open seas adventures, and the occasional pirate.

STANDALONE BOOKS

Ignite Me - A spicy wolf shifter story featuring a lost heir, the mate who doesn't want her, and the enemies who wish them dead.

Marked Paradox - A Young Adult fae story about a realm divided and one fae to bring them back together.

About the Author

Heather Renee is a USA Today Bestselling author who lives in Oregon. She writes Paranormal Romance and Urban Fantasy novels with a mixture of romance, humor, and sass. Her love of reading eventually led to her passion of writing and giving the gift of escapism.

When Heather's not writing, she's spending time with her loving husband and beautiful daughter, going on their own adventures. She loves to hear from her fans, so visit her website: www.HeatherReneeAuthor.com and check out the Contact Me page for ways to connect.